Pillywiggin

The Lost Shadow Boys

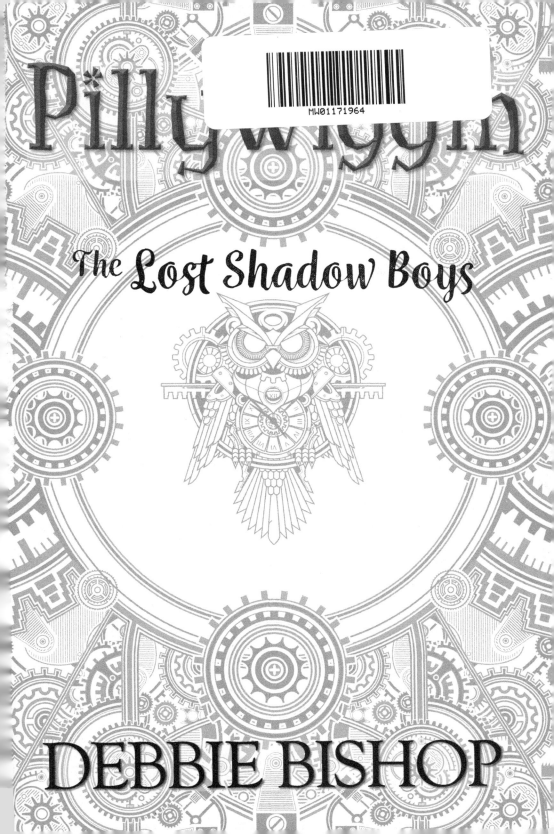

DEBBIE BISHOP

PILLYWIGGIN™
The Lost Shadow Boys
By Debbie Bishop

This is an updated and revised version of the story.

Book design: dbdesign.graphics
Interior illustrations: the-sastra, kixckcore-freepik

Published by:
Angelgate

Printed in the USA

Believe in yourself,
Opportunities will come.
Be ready.

PREQUEL

A shadowy figure carrying a small parcel runs frantically through the night forest through sheets of rain. Stepping clumsily into puddles he searches for a path in blasts of light streaming from a fierce battle overhead. Wails and screams echo admidst the sound of dragon wings and fire, causing the figure to run faster. The forest ignites in light and dark contrasts as the fighting crashes violently to a crescendo, then stops. The forest is suddenly pitch black and eerily silent. A shot of lightening shocks him to losing his grip and the parcel drops and rolls in the mud. He feels around for the parcel but, when he recognizes the loud, slow, flapping sound of the wings of a large fire-breathing dragon growing closer, he runs off.

The dragon uses his fire to light the ground in search of something. As it nears, a pair of young hands gently pull the parcel into the shadows.

Tash, an Indian boy about five years old, bolts through the darkness with the parcel clutched carefully under his arm. Making sure he is unseen, he quietly enters a camoflagued door in a treetrunk. Running down a familar tunnel, he finally climbs steps and exits out another door entering his secret hideaway. Now that he is safe, he takes a long breath, and unwraps the parcel revealing a toddler with large eyeglasses and a toothless grin. Tash brushes a little mud from her hair and is startled to discover a red birthmark on her neck.

"I've seen that...somewhere," he whispers, searching through his belongings. He finds a tattered page that had been torn from a book and compares the mark.

"It's a match." He looks back at the paper and mumbles to himself, "Whosoever bears this mark is of great importance to the realm..."

Gazing softly at the wiggly girl he tells her, "You're the one. When you grow up, you'll be able to break the evil spells on this place." Then he pauses and says solemnly, "If you fail Hagla, the wicked witch of the Heatherworld will take over."

The toddler is more interested in the feather dangling from his hair.

Tash tickles her tummy, "I guess I'll have to keep an eye on you."

CHAPTER 1

10 YEARS LATER

That morning started out like the others. I knew I wasn't supposed to fly over the town, but I liked watching people come out of their houses and open their stores. The warm smell of fresh baked bread and apple-cinnamon tarts smelled like home – or at least what I imagined a real home would be like. I knew better than to let anyone see me, Tashuhunka had warned me, many times. Penstemon was a quaint village with cozy cottages, blossoming flower baskets and cobblestone streets nestled in the rolling hills of the northern tip of Delaware, U.S. The founders, legend has it, had stowed away on a ship, The Half Moon, which was bound for Asia, but when the captain got lost and ended up in Delaware, they made the best of it. The townspeople had forgotten the tragedy that occurred after losing their epic battle and more importantly, what came before it. If I had known then what I know now... well, isn't that what people always say when something has gone terribly wrong?

I flew high enough to be taken for a bird and in fact, so high that my shadow normally did not touch the ground until I passed over the Palace of Penstemon. The fairy castle towered over the cozy town of Penstemon, Penstemon forest, a lovely pond, and way off, on the far side - a trailer park village called Bladderwhack.

That day, however, I didn't make it past the bakery. I was compelled by the intoxicating fragrance of cinnamon and warm baked goodness. Within moments I had climbed in through the back window of the bakery and opened the door behind the counter, just enough to peek inside.

The baker, Mrs. B, which was short for Baglesnitch, was outside on the patio, wiping dew off the tops of cafe tables.

I don't know how long I crouched behind the display case. The glass was steamy from the warmth of muffins and sweet-smelling breads. I was mesmerized. Thankfully, the DING of an oven timer woke me up.

I placed two dollars and change by the cash register, then picked up a potholder and reached for the oven door. The sound of footsteps crept toward me.

"Is someone there?" Mrs. B said glancing my way. I darted for the back window. The money I left by the cash register, and the two missing muffins, caught her eye. I snuck out just in time. Or so I thought. Tash caught me. He was red-faced and huffing so much his exhales steamed up the chilly air around him.

"How many times have I warned you not to go to town without me?" Tash seemed to always be angry back then.

"I got you one."

He yanked me out the window and straight up into the sky.

Tash, his real name was Tashuhunka, but who has time to say all that? I called him Tash. Anyway, he took care of me in those days. Kind of like a mad dad, even though he was only a few years older than me. He had the most beautiful, angular wings that fell behind him like a cape and his shiny black hair was tied back and decorated with a single eagle feather. He was the last living member of his tribe. He never stayed mad at me for very long. It was like anger was a disguise. He never did anything to hurt me. The opposite in fact. He was my protector. All it ever took was a wide smile to bring the sparkle back in his eyes.

We stopped above the clouds, using them for cover from the town.

"Fly above me," he huffed, lightening up a little when I placed a warm muffin in his hand. We flew in unison barely making a shadow on the rooftops. Townspeople below, greeted each other politely as they went about their business.

"I don't see what is so dangerous."

"Rules are made for a reason," Tash warned.

Tash was extra cautious as we glided over the guards of Penstemon Palace. We zig-zagged so our shadow combined with dark crevices in the architecture. As soon as we reached Penstemon Forest I split off, gliding lower through the trees.

I was told that flying through the forest was more dangerous than flying over the town. I didn't see how. Below, the woods were so thick with trees and bushes that I had swerve to avoid them. Okay, so maybe I did fly too fast, especially for a girl my age. I was seven then. About seven, I guess. It was a game to me. I liked watching my shadow flicker in the filtered sunlight and changing levels, flying high and low, staying in shadows and playing with the light – being invisible.

Traveling over the pond was my least favorite part. I was goofy looking. The Indian-style that Tash braided my hair in made me look like a boy. My clothes were, well, his. Tailored for me, but nothing like the beautiful designer dresses all the girls in Penstemon wore. But the worst of it was my glasses. I was the only person in the realm who wore glasses and they were much too large for my face. I didn't really mind. I mean, I like being able to see. I just didn't want to look at myself in the glistening reflection of the pond. So, I normally flew backwards, toes first, disrupting the surface of the water with a ripple that resembled a fun house mirror. Sometimes I crashed on the beach on the other side, but I learned to roll out of it.

I always took a deep breath before I flew to the top of the rocky hill on the southern tip of the pond. It was like I was gathering my courage. This edge of the forest bordered a hellish place known as the Heatherworld. The lands were protected by a force field dome keeping what was inside the dome from getting out. The force field kept us from getting in too, although it didn't have to. No one in their right mind would even try it. The atmospheric disturbance of the force field reflected the sunrise, making it pretty in sharp contrast to the barren landscape inside. Crows and dragons circled above the rock and bone filled valley where an eerie, twisted castle spiraled up from the center.

"What are you doing? Do you have a death wish today?" Tash was genuinely angry. So much that his voice cracked.

"I told you to stay away from here. How many times do I have to warn you?"

"What's the harm? You said yourself they can't get out."

"They'll see you." "So?"

I was drawn to it. I never told him that, and I knew better than to get too close. From inside the force field dome, a disheveled, underfed crow eyed me as if I was dinner. Tash pulled me back into the woods but as he did, I couldn't take my eyes off the Twisted Castle. It was creepy. Every day that I flew by it, chills went up my spine. Still, every day, I snuck up to look at it. I couldn't help it. It was like it was calling to me.

Little did I know the real mystery wasn't the Twisted Castle, it was what lived beneath it.

CHAPTER 2

A crashing rock narrowly missed the head of LB, a small four-year old boy, as he jumped over a lava stream between craggy stalagmite formations running from a ferocious dragon-like lizard intent on catching its breakfast.

This was the Mantlerealm. Thousands of feet below the deathly surface of the Heatherworld, it was an unlikely place to find anyone, especially a child.

LB evaded the beast with skill not normal for one so young. He was scared but determined. The beast leapt at him glaring viciously and opened its enormous warted, snarling jaws.

LB raced, avoiding lava springs that splattered into a lava river that snaked around boulders. The lava's fiery mantle reflected off of gems, shimmering veins of gold crystals and shiny rocks, that lit the tunnel with a yellow-orange glow. The menacing creature's massive feet cracked the ground as it chased its prey. LB glanced back at the charging beast, then grinned.

Jayce, a confident-looking boy about eight-years old, swooped in on an oversized winged skateboard, a "skatewing", flying hard and fast to catch LB first.

Jayce swung to avoid a rock formation, then snatched LB in the middle of a 360, just before the beast's teeth clamped down on him.

LB laid flat, clinging to the board as Jayce circled to exit with the beast chasing them through lava unscathed. Jayce surfed the air like a wave, peddling to flap the wings, then gliding and spiraling to avoid the beast. He was in a foul mood.

"The tunnel is a secret," he said irritably.

"I'm sorry Jayce," LB said nervously. "I wanted to go home."

"We all do," Jayce scowled. "But we'll do it together. You know her rule. If one escapes the rest of us are toast."

The beast was gaining on them. Jayce jumped onto its back and swung a knotted rope under its jaw. He pulled back hard, lifting its head up, then twisted it sideways, knocking it out. The beast tumbled to a stop, slamming Jayce into the wall.

Jayce pried himself loose, then ran ahead of the skatewing, leapt off a rock and somersaulted, landing lightly, back on his board. He gasped at the sight of greenish light shining in from ahead then aimed for a ledge near the ceiling, just before it.

"Get back to the cave," he whispered urgently to LB. "I'll deal with the witch.

LB jumped onto the ledge landing without making a sound, pushed open a hidden rock door, then scrambled through it.

Jayce swallowed his feeling of dread and flew forward doing a triple spiral before buzzing a squadron of heavily armed Oddizen guards. He stopped abruptly when Hagla, the wicked witch of the Heatherworld, turned the corner in a chariot flown by her two favorite dragons. This was not the first time he found himself face to flame-tip with these thugs. The Black Dragon and Zenuvius were the largest and most feared of the witch's mercenary dragons.

Jayce never let his fear show. Especially with Zenuvius. The rivalry between them was interesting to Zenuvius and from past run ins, Jayce had convinced himself that courage, even if he was faking it, was what kept him alive. Not even the dragon chief had authority to kill any of the boys, but Jayce knew an accident by the hag's fave pet would be forgiven.

Zenuvius and the Black Dragon landed and closed in on him menacingly as the Oddizens - mystical creatures born or created from combined species - swarmed around Jayce pointing their weapons at him. Jayce stood still, as if he knew this routine.

Hagla was viciously delighted.

"Jayson, why is it that you are the only boy who ever tries to escape?" She cackled. Even petrified, Jayce's charisma shined.

"The only thing I'm trying to escape is being that

Oddizen's breakfast," he replied cockily.

The witch got out of her carriage and slithered to him. "You don't think I know you cover for the little ones?" Hagla gleamed. "Finding it difficult to keep them in line?"

"You've got a lot of rules to remember." Jayce was trying hard to conceal his hatred of her because he knew all that would do is put him in more trouble. She did have many rules and penalties for breaking them. Inflicting pain on others is what she lived for, and today Jayce had given her an extra treat.

"I think I can help you with that," Hagla smiled. She plucked a hair from his head and studied it. Then she looked deep into his eyes as if she was searching his soul. After a tense moment she put the hair into a velvet pouch and climbed back into her carriage. "It is time to put an end to your mischief."

"Take him to the tower," she bellowed to the guards.

The next thing Jayce saw was a huge fist in his face.

"No. There must be another way," a hushed voice said with urgency. It startled me. The words seemed to hang in the air. I will never forget that afternoon. My life changed. I had been playing with bunnies in a flowery grassy meadow... what? Hey, I was seven. When I returned to our camp, Tash was sitting by the stream, dreamwalking. Up until then, I had only seen him do it at night. He had his back to me, but I could tell by the way he was swaying...and the fact that he didn't hear me come up behind him, that he was deep into it.

Tashuhunka was a mighty Indian even at age twelve. His black-veined wings, and strong, regal stance, made him seem commanding. But this day was different. He was slumped over. Tash never slumped.

He heard my last step and straightened up.

"How's your grandfather?" I asked. Tash's grandfather was his spirit guide.

"You do know he's dead?"

I had never seen him in such a serious mood. He didn't even turn around when he said it.

"Nothing ever really dies," I said softly as I knelt beside him. "What did he tell you today?"

Tash's face was wet with tears.

"What's wrong?"

He got up without looking at me and hurriedly packed my things into a satchel.

"I found you a new place to live," Tash said sharply.

"Why can't I stay with you?"

He looked at me with such sad eyes. Then, looking up, he noticed the position of the sun in the sky. "It's time. They're coming," he said solemnly.

"Who?"

"Tell them you are the girl from the letter."

"But you were going to help me find my parents?"

"We don't always get what we want, Chloe," he snarled. "Your parents are not searching for you."

"Yes, they are." I snarled back.

"Think about it. If they are alive, they know who you are."

I must have looked confused because he answered my question before I asked it.

"You are the only orphan in Penstemon and the only one who wears big eyeglasses."

"You think my glasses are too big?"

"Why do you always twist my words?" he huffed and stomped toward a meadow.

We were never great at communicating. But honestly, arguing about nothing was better than admitting the truth. Tash was right. My parents HAD to know where I was. Maybe not the secret camp where Tash and I lived—it was camouflaged pretty well—but I had gone to town occasionally for the annual town parties where there were so many people you could get lost in the crowd. So, some people knew me. I wanted to think my parents were alive... just not about why they hadn't looked for me.

The sound of the birds scattering away startled me back to reality. Tash was glaring at me with his mouth open like, WHAT?

"You're daydreaming again. Don't daydream in the middle of a conversation. People will think you're an idiot."

"What people?"

He suddenly became very serious.

A kind-looking man, Pops, and his daughter Tip, a girl with short red hair from my class, walked toward us in the distance. Tash moved quickly into the shadows of the trees. He always stayed out of sight when people were around.

"What are they doing here?" I didn't really want to know. My stomach turned over and I felt sick.

"I wrote them a letter, or you did. I signed your name. You like her, right? Tip."

"Yes, but."

"Chloe, it has to be this way."

"But I live here."

"Not any more. Go on," he said sternly.

"No," I clung to him. "You are my home."

He softened up and held me tightly.

"It is time to grow up," Tash whispered. "It's okay, I will always protect you." Then, he let me go.

I didn't look at him again. I couldn't. I didn't want him to see me cry. I knew he thought this was best for me. He was my best friend, but I wasn't a little kid anymore. I was a girl and he was a boy. I thought that he cared for me too much and that is why he found me a new home.

I had no idea how clueless I was.

Jayce gasped quietly in pain when he pulled the lever on the hand-made shower in the cave that was his bedroom. The small dark cavern was lit by a lantern that sat next to a makeshift bed on a dirt floor. He cringed when the water hit his skin, then clenched his teeth, and washed the blood off in silence.

Just outside, LB ran past, dodging dirty-faced boys as he scurried through small caverns of a larger cave that was lit by handmade lanterns.

"He's here," LB whispered excitedly.

Two older boys, Beav, big and wide, and Leo, a blond

surfer type, shuffled in around a large boulder that sheltered the main cavern from the entrance to the cave. Exhausted and sweaty, the boys dropped mining tools into a metal box and took their heavy shoes off. LB's words perked them up. "He's here."

In an offshoot cavern, water dripped from the ceiling in a slow-flowing waterfall. Boys stood in a puddle under it, barefoot but in clothes, washing themselves. Run-off from the shower was diverted through screens that funneled the water into a shallow channel about the size of a pipe that was carved into the stone floor.

LB grinned wide at Parker, age seven, who looked like a monster showering with his goggles on and his hair askew.

Next to him, Max, about five, bare-chested with angular, masculine translucent wings, laid his shirt on a rock to dry. Max shook his head and his hair POOFED into a loosely curled afro much too big for his skinny frame. He flicked his wings and they tucked in, disappearing under the skin on his back.

Hushed excitement passed between boys who stopped what they were doing when they heard LB, then they rushed to the center cavern and sat expectantly.

Max and Parker sat down in the front next to Beav and Leo as LB grabbed Grimly – a big-eyed bug about the size of his hand. When he tapped its butt, Grimly glowed a warm yellow. LB handed him to Max who put the bug into a lantern in front of him, and then, they waited.

In the dark offshoot cave that was his room, Jayce sat

on his bed using a hand-held mirror to see a wound on his forehead. He pulled his hair over it when Tash entered.

"You can't keep taking their beatings for them."

"They're kids," Jayce pretended he didn't hurt as badly as he did. "So are you."

"You want to switch places... any time's fine with me."

"You know I would," Tash said sincerely.

"Yeah, I know."

"Where's the aloe I brought?" Tash asked.

Jayce nodded to the bed behind him. "That's the last of it."

Tash picked up the salve and smeared it gently on the wounds on Jayce's back. Jayce tried not to cringe from the sting but, couldn't help it.

"What's that?"

Jayce shifted his body trying to conceal a book that was lying on his pillow. He dreaded the lecture he was about to get from his over-protective friend.

"Nothin'. Just a book."

"You stole from the witch?"

"She took something from me," Jayce grunted with hushed anger.

LB entered excitedly catching Jayce off-guard. Tash leaned into the light, shielding him nonchalantly while Jayce picked up a shirt to hide his wounds from LB. Still, the boy caught a glimpse.

"Do you hurt?" he asked with concern.

"I'm fine," Jayce lied, smiling. "Tash is going to tell

you a long one today."

Tash understood the cue. "I brought oranges," he told LB with a grin. "Will you pass them out for me?"

"You bet!" LB exclaimed and he ran out to get them.

Tash picked up bandages of cloth and carefully helped Jayce wrap his hands. "We've got to get you guys out of here."

"It's no use," Jayce's out-of-character pessimism caught Tash by surprise.

"You're giving up?"

"No. I'm giving in," Jayce said angrily. He was so scared he was seething. "We'll wait for the prophecy."

Something had switched in him. He put fingerless work gloves on to hide his bandages and opened and closed his bloodied fist, straining to control the pain.

"We will get out of here," he mumbled. "We will plan and train and when Chloe comes for us, we'll be ready."

Tash had never seen him more angry or determined. "What happened? What did Hagla take from you?"

"She cursed me." Jayce glared.

Tash was alarmed.

"She took me to the castle and made a dark faery spell with a strand of my hair, and sealed it with a strap from my pants. Now, one wrong move and I'm done." Jayce exhaled hard with frustration. "There's gotta be something in that book on how to reverse the spell."

"The book's on magic? You know magic doesn't work down here."

"Hers does. I thought I could learn to use it, but I can

barely make out the handwriting."

"Handwritten? You mean this is a journal?" Tash gasped and very carefully picked it up. "Jayce. This is the seal of Lord Darkshadow."

"Who's that?"

"He was the leader of the dark faeries and pretty much all things evil. You think Hagla's bad, Lord Darkshadow was a million times worse."

"Was?"

"He was murdered."

"By who? The witch?"

"Dunno." Tash leafed through the pages cautiously. "This is dangerous stuff. You can't mess with black magic. It will turn you."

"What does it matter?" Jayce snatched the book from Tash and slid it under his blanket. "The hag's got me now. We're never getting out. I can't do anything to disobey her."

"Except steal a journal of the darkest spells on the planet." Tash is suddenly suspicious. "She knows everything that goes on in the Twisted Castle."

"You think she wanted me to have it? What, to turn me?" Jayce becomes pale. Tash had never seen him so desperate.

"We'll think of something, okay?" Tash said softly.

"Yeah, well think fast. I'm freaking out here."

"No kiddin'."

Outside, in the main cavern, the boys gasped with gleeful whispers when Tash walked into their circle.

"You guys ready for Bingo?" he teased. Max's jaw dropped.

"What? No."

That made everyone laugh, including the bug. Tash glanced at four boys standing guard and put his finger to his lips. The other boys quieted immediately.

"You know the story we want to hear," LB whispered.

"The evil one and her quest for the throne," Parker added excitedly.

Tash took a master storyteller stance and began.

"Dragonfire lit up the night sky. Light Fairies and their fairydragons had battled Hagla, the wicked witch of the Heatherworld and her mercenary dragon army into the wee hours just before dawn."

The boys closed their eyes and imagined short blasts of light flashing in the night sky over Penstemon Palace and its colorful town as fire-breathing dragons violently thrashed at smaller fairydragons and elderfairies.

"Hagla had blackmailed the thirteen members of the Ancient Council into making her next in line for Emperor Drescil's throne. She had discovered a secret about them and thought it would be enough to get her the crown. But Emperor Drescil broke with tradition and chose a different heir. When a spy told her, the witch had a fit. She snapped the reins of her open carriage – pulled by two of the mightiest fire-breathing dragons on earth – and blazed to Fairydom Castle in Scotland to find out if the rumor was true."

Tash crouched down and leaned in for effect.

"People ran for cover when Zenuvius melted the royal gates with his flame and then pulled her carriage right up to the castle doors. Members of Fairydom Court were too afraid to look at her. It was a well-known fact that Hagla delighted in zapping people into crinkly black bugs, so they looked down, not saying a word as she blasted by them toward the Emperor. Drescil was unafraid. He looked the hag right in the eyes, and boldly told her that in accordance with the Laws of the Royal League she was disqualified due to her use of black magic."

"Then he zapped her out on her boney butt," LB said laughing. His giggle was infectious.

Parker shushed them and Tash continued.

"But the witch came back. One of the ancients told her that she could have the title if the young heir willfully gave up his claim."

Jayce walked gingerly to the circle. Tash looked the boys in the eyes, catching their gaze as Jayce slowly sat down next to him.

"Problem was, Drescil and his Royal Secret Service, the RSS, had kept the child's identity so secret that no one, not the parents, not even the heir himself knew who the lucky guy was." He paused for dramatic effect.

"Hagla did the unthinkable. She broke into Fairydom's private Royal Library, which at the time, was the most highly guarded vault on earth. Disguised as Judith, the Supreme Fairy and Guardian of the Light, she tricked the minions into giving her the sacred golden scroll that named the young emperor-to-be. Even the evil hag gasped at its significance when she held it in her crinkled, clammy hands. This little heir, when they came of age and passed the challenges would be given all of Emperor Drescil's power and wisdom, and one day reign over all realms and mystical creatures on earth. But," Tash continues with emphasis, "a tiny minion, so small the hag had overlooked him, saw the witch's ugly true reflection in a mirror and alerted the guards. RSS agents rushed in but with one flick of her finger the witch's black magic knocked them out cold. She zapped the minion into a black bug then opened the scroll. She had what she came for. She read the name of the province where the heir lived. PENSTEMON. The town of Penstemon shared a border with her own lands. She wondered if the Ancients had a made it easy for her or, if Drescil had actually found a regal match in the spirit of a child here. Fortunately, just before she could read the name of the heir...someone sneezed on the scroll and the ink ran together."

"That's my favorite part," LB laughed as he held his knees and rocked back and forth. "Shhh," Tash warned. He looked back at the boy standing guard by the boulder. The boy nodded it was clear.

"So, the witch didn't know who the lucky little guy was," Tash continued with hushed enthusiasm. "She zapped out in a dark magical dust cloud just as the Royal Secret Service arrived with reinforcements. The Emperor knew she wouldn't stop there. He sent Judith to warn the fairies of Penstemon that Hagla was on her way home to start a war and he even sent RSS operatives to help them fight, but they were doomed from the start. The witch had been diverting fairy dust for months and she had recruited the most vicious mercenary dragons in the world for her army. Fairydragons were no match for them and without magic the good fairies couldn't defend themselves. They were dropping like flies. Penstemon's King Kenneth organized the ground forces while Queen Rose supervised the rescue medical teams who picked up the injured and brought them to the makeshift hospital they had set up in the palace courtyard. The good fairies put up a valiant effort, but it wasn't long before there were only two creatures left to defend against Hagla and her army. Judith, and her loyal friend Hal, who was now the last Fairydragon. Hagla and Judith blasted each other with magic so powerful it shook the sky."

Tashuhunka straightened up, flaring his masculine wings, powerfully raised his arms for dramatic effect, then imitated Hagla's high-pitched crackly voice.

"'Tell me the name of the boy, Judith or I will destroy this town and everyone in it.' Hagla bellowed. Judith sang back, 'I will find out what hold you have over the ancients, Hagla, and I will stop you. You will never rule Fairydom.' Judith blasted her. Hagla pretended she was hurt and used Judith's pause of empathy to snatch her wand. Then she popped Judith into a cage."

Tash became more animated, hopping on top of a rock for effect as he imitated the characters.

"You're such a sap,' the witch cackled. 'Save your pity

for yourself, doll-face, you're trapped like a bird. Zenuvius, take over. Akasha, Seurillilious, come with me."

"Hal hovered on top of Judith's cage, and said, 'Touch one hair on her head and I'll mortalize ya.'"

"Yeah? You and what army?" Tash slurred sinisterly with a Russian accent imitating Zenuvius. "Look around you, Fairydragon. You lose."

Tash raised his voice for Judith's whisper, "Hal, stay with the boys.' That made Hagla laugh, he said. 'Stay with the boys Hal. HA! Honey, stick a fork in him, he's done. My dragons will eat him for breakfast. Tell me the name of the heir Judith. You know I'll find him. Then all creatures will bow down to me.' Judith sang her last words, 'You can't win, Hagla. Good always prevails in fairytales.' Hagla sneered, 'You do notice you're in a cage dear? I win. Say bye-bye.'"

A shadow shifted behind Tash.

"Hal raged. Zenuvius took one look at him and flamed Hal's head. Hal snooted, 'You know they make medicine for acid reflux these days.' The comedian wanna-be was half the size of the carnivorous mercenary, and with tiny, little fairywings, but he moved fast, like a boxer. Zenuvius couldn't keep up, mostly because he was laughing too hard."

A large figure stepped silently from the shadows into the light. It was Hal, the last fairydragon, creeping up on Tash. His hot breath in Tash's ear made him jump.

"AHH!" Tash covered his scream with his hand then shook his head at Hal.

"There is no need to use both tiny and little in the

same sentence. Especially in describing my wings," Hal huffed.

Tash grinned at him.

"Jayce was the first to get nabbed." Tash tossed a sly glance at Jayce needling his friend. "His screams echoed in the night as the Zenuvius carried him away from his room above Mrs. B's bakery."

"Like I was the only one screaming that night. Besides, I was what, four?"

"Will you guys get on with it?" LB huffed impatiently.

"You know this story," Jayce laughed.

"Yeah, but he's getting to the best part," LB replied. He closed his eyes, imagining as Tash retold the story.

"Hal, surrounded by a crowd of mercenary dragons, watched helplessly as Judith was whisked away into the dark mist. Ickadorus, Icky for short – a tiny orange and yellow dragon with a size complex, noticed Hal's wings. 'A dragon named Hal? Where's the flair in that? It's one syllable. And what the heck are those things? Why even my wings are bigger than yours. Zenuvius bellowed, 'No wonder the fairies lose. You have sissy girlie fairy wings.'"

"Yes," Hal huffed, "But they look so much better under a coat, less of a hump."

The boys laughed as silently as they could.

"Zenuvius let Hal live, obviously," Tash said solemnly, "but he was helpless to stop them. All he could do is watch as the dragon squads took all the boys away from their homes. Meanwhile, in the Palace of Penstemon, Prince Peter was smuggled out by RSS agents. A Royal escort lead by Lt. Knockins, a two-headed frog gentleman, an Oddizen to be sure, snuck in from a secret door in the fireplace."

LB opened his eyes.

"That's the night you found Chloe," he said.

"Yes. The dragon squad spotted me in the town. I lost them in the forest. That's when I saw Chloe tumbling down a muddy bank."

"Tash's grandfather predicted it," Jayce interrupted.

"Are you telling this story or am I?" Tash miffed.

"I'll take it from here." Jayce and Tash were best friends, but both wanted to be leader.

LB, Max, Parker, Beav and Leo huddled close to the lantern, waiting. Other boys were strewn about on the dirt floor of the cave, listening, half-asleep.

Jayce lowered his voice ominously. "It was a rainy night. There hadn't been a storm like that in the history of the world. Baby Chloe sat in Tash's teepee as he shuffled through pages trying to read in flashes of lightning."

"Hey, I wasn't that lame. I had a flashlight."

"Okay, whatever. Anyway, according to the ancient prophecies, one fairy would have the power break the witch's evil spells and free us. Had Tashuhunka found THAT fairy? She had the mark on her neck his grandfather had told him about. The crest of Fairydom, no less. Tash made a solemn vow, to himself, right then, to protect her from that point on. He found a family of bunnies to take her in." Jayce stared at Tash disapprovingly. "Bunnies? Why?"

Tash straightened up, defending himself.

"No one would look for her there. The dragon squads were going door to door. People hadn't forgotten yet. Besides, the bunnies were warm and fluffy."

"Ok-aay," Jayce rolled his eyes.

"How does he know his grandfather? His whole tribe is dead." Max asked bluntly.

"Max, I'm right here."

"Tash's grandfather was a great medicine man," Jayce whispered dramatically.

"Can you teach us to dreamwalk?" LB asked.

"I taught Jayce. I guess if he can learn it anyone can." Tash laughed. Jayce smirked at him.

"Why do you hide in the woods?" Beav asked.

Jayce answered for Tash. "So Hagla's spies don't catch him and toss him in here with us.

"What's legendary?" Max inquired.

"He stays out of sight," Parker said matter-of-factly. "People think he's a myth. Only a few, besides us, have ever seen him."

"Why didn't Chloe's parents come and get her?" Leo asked thoughtfully.

"They might have been killed in the battle," Parker says.

"Do you know who the heir to the emperor's throne is?" Beav interrupted.

"I don't even think he knows," Tash replied.

"Is it Chloe?" LB asked.

"Doubtful. It could be one of you guys."

"No way it's you, Beav," Max teased.

"You think you're Drescil's pick?" Beav bellowed.

"You're both dreaming," Parker reminded them. "Peter's the one that got away. The emperor's agents rescued him."

"Why didn't they rescue us?" Leo wondered.

"They tried," Jayce said softly, "but our side lost."

"Man, I would love to see that two headed Oddizen dude!" Leo quiffed. "Does he have conversations with himself?"

"That's what you think about?" Beav shook his head. The boys laughed.

They were getting too loud. Jayce interrupted. "Do you want to hear the rest of this story or not?"

"We want Tash to tell it," LB mumbled.

"Fine."

Tash grinned, then, used his hands to emulate magic.

"Hagla cast three spells," he said eerily. "First, she erased all memory of the boys. Images of happy children vanished before their parents' eyes. Parker's parents watched in wonder as his bedroom changed into a den with a TV and a crafts area. As soon as his dad laid eyes on the remote it was over, Parker who? Beav's parents were ecstatic over the new power lawn mower the witch made from his big wheel and Leo's dad forgot he was even carrying Leo's skateboard and butt pads when they disappeared."

Tash looked around, hopeful his teasing had lightened

the reality of it. LB was trying so hard not to laugh that he had turned completely red and looked about to explode. Finally, he couldn't contain it.

"AHH-ah-ah!" he blurted. "Butt-pads!"

Leo surprised him with a shove that knocked him over.

LB grinned at Leo and snickered in a really low voice. "Butt-pads," he giggled at Leo teasingly.

Tash continued. "Pops opened the cupboard drawer that was LB's bed, put a loaf of bread inside and thought nothing more about it. Mrs. B started her successful bakery the day Jayce's photo was replaced with a blue ribbon for the world's best bagels. But the happiest moment was when Max's mom found his room had changed into a new walk-in closet."

"Hey, my mom's got taste," Max gloated proudly. "She's gotta have a place to put all her 'this n that', you know?"

"By morning, the town and you guys had disappeared from the world." Tash said solemnly. "Words about that night, the boys or the war would be heard as jibberish and instantly forgotten. Hagla had stolen all the fairy dust and her spell made magic of any substance without it, useless. Then, the town was sealed off and forgotten. No one in, and no one out. The only good thing was that Judith cast a force field spell over Hagla's land before she was captured. When the hag went home, she and her army were trapped inside. Never to bother anyone in Penstemon or outside her lands, again."

"Where's Judith now?" Leo wondered.

"I wish I knew."

"How's Chloe? When is she coming to get us?" Being the littlest, LB was the most optimistic of the group. He yawned and then laid down to hear the rest of the story.

"Chloe moved to a new home in Bladderwhack," Tash told them stiffly, not looking forward to getting back to an empty camp.

Max was shocked. Not in a good way.

"Bladderwhack? The trailerpark? How uncool is that?"

Tash stood up. If he stayed much longer it would be dangerous for him. "The point is she's safe. She'll come into her powers soon."

"And then that old witch will get what's comin'." LB imagined a superhero version of Chloe whacking Hagla around the mines with super strength and lasers shooting from her eyes. "And we'll all go home."

"Sure, LB." Jayce said softly, covering him with a patchwork blanket. "Just like you said."

CHAPTER 3

PRESENT DAY

The secret section of the boys' cave is refurbished to the point of a functional home—proof that they, now in their teens, have not wasted a moment in their horrific prison. Handmade chairs, tables, beds and lanterns are placed in an organized fashion. Pipes made from rocks run along the ceiling carrying water to faucets with hand carved shut off valves. For a cave, it is polished and clean—even comfortable, but with a definite sense of danger. In the front three sections of the cave, no one speaks above a whisper. Boys near the entrance sharpen tools but they are actually on the look out for guards. Aware that the witch may be watching through a camera she had set up outside, boys take shifts going about their daily routines in the stark outer chambers. She does allow them privacy for personal hygiene and they used that space to chisel their way through the rock and into the hidden inner tunnels where they made their real home. But even tucked away where no one can see them, they are on constant alert.

Near the rear of their cave, boys quietly hone their flying skills over obstacles they set up. The cavern isn't very large. They flip at the walls like they are doing laps in a pool. They are for the most part, orderly and polite with each other, but every one of them is suppressing a searing anger toward their oppressors that has reached its boiling point.

Leo, tall and athletic with shoulder length blond hair and zen-like calmness that seems out of place here, runs up a wall, leaps backwards into a kicking spiral back flip and lands without making a sound. The rock he kicks with his bare foot splits in half and falls silently into soft dirt.

Max wheels a tarp-covered cart into the main cavern from the rear. Almost seventeen now, he is still skinny but the work in the mines has made his thin body more muscular than normal for a boy his age. His grin says it all. Boys excitedly rush the cart and push each other out of the way to be first to pull the tarp off.

"Tash brought oranges!"

Leo reaches over a shorter boy and grabs two oranges tossing one to the bug. "Grimly, heads up."

Grimly peels it with a knife, like a gentleman.

Beav, tallest of the bunch and a foot wider, tackles Leo knocking the rickety cart over. They fall to the ground and oranges pile on top of them creating a frenzied free-for-all. Laughter fills the room – for a moment.

"Shhh!" Max tries to stop laughing but it just makes it worse.

A rumbling sound alarms them. All eyes look toward

the entrance of the cave. Parker, in full mining gear, pushes back his goggles as he runs in with a worried expression.

"Where's Jayce?"

The urgency in his voice can only mean one thing. Someone is in trouble. Here, someone is always in trouble.

"Sleeping. Finally. What's up?" Leo says.

Parker takes a step toward Jayce's chamber.

Leo stops him. "Don't wake him. The dude's been up for three days."

Parker ignores him.

Although dark, Jayce's room is about as nice as a cave dwelling can get. The floor is covered in polished slate. A trunk carved from stone sits next to his simple cot-like bed. Jayce sleeps on top of his blanket, with his shirt off, dreaming.

⁕

That was the first time I saw him. He was standing just outside my classroom window, staring at me. I had no idea who he was, or what I was doing there. I guess I had fallen asleep in class. Our gaze met and the next thing I knew was I had stepped out of my body and was being drawn to this guy... A guy. I felt as if I knew him, but that was impossible. I mean, there weren't any boys in Penstemon, well, except Tash, but he didn't really count. I couldn't stop myself. Some unseen force sucked me right through the wall. I guess in spirit form you can do things like that. But there I was, suddenly, looking into his eyes, close enough to kiss and feeling like I wanted to. The chemistry between us was so strong, I was afraid to touch him.

"Chloe."

How did he know my name? I was so frightened I couldn't speak.

"Why haven't you come for us?" I think that's what he said. He said it so softly, I didn't completely understand.

"Who are you?" I don't think I said it, I thought it. No wonder he didn't answer. Why did he feel so familiar to me?

He was about to touch my hand when an agonized look came over his face. It terrified him. The air behind him started to blur like a black hole. He reached for me and grabbed my hands. I held on as tightly as I could but the force pulling at him was too strong. The blur swirled into a tunnel. I could feel his fear. He screamed silently until he faded out.

Moments later I was back at my desk, awake. I honestly didn't know if what just happened was just a daydream, or if it was real. It felt real. Then I noticed my hands. The depressions of his grasp on my skin lingered for several seconds before they disappeared.

Jayce wakes up to see Parker rushing in.

"LB?" Jayce knows the answer. Sitting, he slips his shoes on before he stands up. "This time it's bad." Parker is more serious than usual.

Jayce clips on an armored vest and buckles the clasp as he exits. Boys shuffle out of his path as he rushes toward a solid rock wall. A boy pulls a hidden lever and a slab opens just enough for Jayce to slip through. Jayce pauses, standing in the shadow of a boulder until the secret door shuts quietly behind him. A glance from another boy tells him it is clear and Jayce rushes urgently past several worried boys to the cave entrance.

Jayce stands at the edge of the Shadow Boys cave and quickly sizes up the scene below him. The Mantlerealm mines are a horrific sight. The steep, hot cavern is scarred by the mining of veins of fairy dust and precious gems. Handmade scaffolding, train tracks, cargo elevators and ropes connect the levels. Lava springs flowing from rock walls feed into mantle streams that weave around sharp boulders at the bottom of the deep ravine.

The boys' cave is at the very top level where it was the coolest. On every other level, troll and Oddizen guards carrying ancient-looking weapons harass boys working the mines. It is too hot to even expose their wings, let alone fly. The boys use makeshift wooden cars, skateboards and gliders to maneuver around the levels. Three guards sneer at Jayce as they ride past him in a flying contraption that is peddled by six boys.

On the main control level an angry group of mystical creatures lead by Wiggins, an Oddizen bat with a bloody scratch on his waist, surround LB, the youngest of the boys at fifteen.

Jayce places an oval shaped board on the ground next to the ledge and clamps its wheels to a rope. When he steps on it, he drops twenty feet immediately. The rope sways under him, but he rides it like a skilled surfer on a massive, shifting wave, across the treacherous ravine to the other side. There, he drops down several levels and runs across a narrow bridge where he jumps on a skateboard with hand-sewn wings and peddles, sailing to the main control station. The scene is chaotic. The chattering crowd closes in on LB. He has never been so scared.

"I'm sorry Wiggins," LB stutters.

"Sorry? You tried to kill me!" Wiggins screeches feverishly, inciting the crowd even more.

"No, I didn't," LB tries to explain. "You flew too close to my knife when I was plucking the gem. Honest, I didn't mean to cut ya."

The crowd separates for Cosentino, a mighty troll with attitude.

"How come whenever there's trouble, you're the cause of it?" Cosentino growls. "It was an accident," LB says defiantly.

"You wanna see an accident?" Cosentino picks LB up with one hand and shakes him over the salivating crowd.

Jayce sails to them valiantly, and then jumps off in front of LB, showing no fear of the fierce troll. "Cosentino. He meant no harm."

"He attacked my men." Cosentino argues.

Jayce's glare is piercing as he leans toward Cosentino, eye to eye. "If LB wanted to harm Wiggins, he would not be alive to whine about it."

"I told ya, I didn't mean it," LB chimes in. "Sure kid,"

Cosentino says sarcastically.

"Look, we fight, the witch will kill us. Then who will mine your precious gems? Face it. You can't run your operation without us." Jayce's tone is soft, but threatening.

Cosentino drops LB and then growls at the mob. "Back to work."

He slams Jayce up against a wall.

"I take it you'd like more production?" Jayce wheezes.

"Put a leash on that kid. Hagla's goon's been pokin' into my business. Last thing we want is for her to come down here again."

"You think she knows you've been stealing from her?"

"How long you think your boys will last without food?" Cosentino is serious. After a tense moment, he lets up on Jayce.

LB jumps onto the skate-wing and pumps the pedals, readying for lift-off. Jayce steps toward it, but the serious glare on Cosentino's face causes him to turn back.

"What is it?" Jayce asks.

Cosentino turns away.

"Cosentino."

Cosentino and Wiggins exchange a knowing glance. "What's going on?" Jayce repeats.

Cosentino doesn't answer. Jayce stares at him until he finally gives in. "You won't like it," he warns.

"Concern? From you? Okay, now you're scaring me." Cosentino pulls Jayce aside, so no one else can hear.

"The Emperor's been sick. The hag thinks he's gonna

pick another heir. Nobody but the ancients remember you guys, and she's got them blackmailed. The only thing she needs you for is the fairy dust and,"

"We're almost at quota."

This is very bad news. Without the need for fairydust, the witch won't need the boys. They'll be expendable, which down here is another word for dragon food.

"Exactly. Just when I was gettin' a soft spot for you."

"Right."

Jayce joins LB on the skatewing. He looks at the boys in the mines as he and LB peddle back to their cave on the top level. He practically raised these guys. Well, basically they raised each other, and they had help from Tash and Hal, but Jayce has been their leader. He kept them alive all these years and even more remarkably, they've grown into men of character and integrity and still have their dream of freedom.

Watching them work as he sails up to their cave, the thought sweeps through him, that now they are going to die. He thinks to himself that he should have let it happen when they first got there. It would have saved them all so much pain.

Boys waiting on scaffolding by the entrance to their cave move to catch the skatewing when Jayce and LB approach. Jayce throws Parker the rope as he lands abruptly and jumps off. LB stumbles when he steps off and then follows him nervously, running to catch up.

CHAPTER 4

Boys, pretending to work, speak quietly into carefully hidden communication devices as Jayce whisks past them. In plain view of the cave entrance, boys on decoy duty sit in stark surroundings looking bored and depressed. Jayce steps slyly behind the large boulder and enters through the secret door to their hidden cave home. He waits until the stone door is shut behind them, then stops and checks LB's wounds.

"You put all of us in danger, LB," Jayce scolds. "We're running out of bribes."

"I'm sorry." LB's chin quivers as he says it.

Jayce softens and tousles his hair. "Hal?"

A large nose leans into the light, followed by the rest of Hal as he bends down to inspect the scrape on LB's hand. "Come with me if you want to live."

His overacted Terminator impression makes LB laugh. Carrying a medical bag, Hal waddles like a big-bottomed nurse toward a water spring in an interior wall. Boys resting beside it chuckle when Hal exaggerates his butt-swing.

"Walk this way."

Beav, surrounded by a mound of orange peels, picks a seed out of his teeth while Leo reaches for the last orange. Beav is faster. He holds it just out of Leo's range, then bites into it, spitting out the rind. One glance at Jayce's stoic expression and Parker knows something is wrong. He follows Jayce toward the back of the cave. Leo jumps to his feet in one swift move. Beav sweeps his arm through Leo's jump, nearly tripping him.

"Too slow." Leo somersaults out of it laughing then follows Parker.

Beav throws the orange at LB. "Ow."

"LB. Heads up. Oops. Sorry bud." Beav gets up.

"Say it before you throw it, Beav. Before." LB miffs.

"I can never remember that," Beav grins, obviously lying. LB takes the orange from his lap and grumbles as he bites into it.

By the time Beav catches up to them, the guys have lost their sense of humor.

"We've got to slow production," Jayce says.

"No problem. I'll put Beav and Leo in charge of the next shift," Parker kids, but the joke falls flat.

Tash steps from behind a boulder. Circumstances have made him a warrior, and he, like Jayce, is in a serious mood.

Parker, Leo and Beav back off.

Tash beats Jayce into his chamber as glow bugs in lanterns light up when they pass.

"We have a problem," Tash states ominously.

"That's what I was going to tell you. If Chloe is going

to do her thing, now would be when to do it."

"That's the problem."

"What do you mean? She should have come into her powers by now." Tash shakes his head.

"She hasn't?" Jayce was shocked.

"I may have been wrong about her." Tash confesses.

"Are you kidding?" Jayce feels like the wind is punched out of him.

"I'm not sure that she is the one."

Jayce glares at Tash angrily.

"You haven't told her about us, have you?"

From Tash's blank expression Jayce knows it is true. He stares at Tash, not wanting to believe it.

"Guards." Parker whispers from the door. The glow bugs instantly go dark Tash disappears in the shadows.

At the cave entrance, Strongarm, an enormous troll with one arm twice the size of the other stands anxiously next to Wiggins who is holding a scanner that counts the boys. They are both shivering and Strongarm's skin is turning blue with frost. The scanner beeps and they hurry outside to the hot mines.

"I don't know how they can stand it so cold. It's freezing in there." Strongarm gruffs. Wiggins speaks into a walky-talky. "All accounted for. Moving on."

A boy outside carefully texts so the guards don't see. Inside their secret chambers, Parker gets the message.

"They're gone." Parker whispers to Jayce from just outside his room.

Jayce finishes removing his clothing revealing a tight black suit underneath as Tash steps back into the light.

"What are you going to do?" Tash asks.

"Oh, like you care now?"

"Of course. There is more to this than you know."

"That I believe." Jayce says angrily.

"Jayce, it's complicated."

"No. It's not. Truth is all we have down here. Good or bad. We have to know what to expect." Jayce steps toward his bedside trunk then turns back toward Tash. "I get it," he says sincerely. "The stories gave them hope. But why lie to me?"

"I didn't lie."

"So you're lying now? Get it straight man." Jayce lifts lid of the trunk open. Lord Darkshadow's journal, now well worn around its edges, is laying on top of a blanket inside. Jayce turns around glaring angrily at Tash. "We were counting on her...because you told us to."

"We'll figure something out."

"How many times have I heard that before?"

"You think it's been easy for me to leave you guys here?"

Jayce looks down trying to control his anger. There isn't time to argue. He has to focus on a solution. "Nevermind. I'll take care of it."

He crouches next to the trunk hiding his face and fights off a surge of darkness that sweeps through his body at the mere decision to go against the witch. He pushes the book aside and reaches under a blanket.

"You can't," Tash warns. "Have you forgotten the curse?"

Jayce stands up and boldly looks at Tash with black eyes. "Must have slipped my mind." Jayce quips.

Tash jumps back.

"Relax. I can control it."

Jayce's eye color returns to normal.

"For how long?" Tash worries.

"Doesn't matter. We're out of options."

"We'll come up with a new plan."

"So you can nix that one at the last second too?" Jayce says angrily. "No thanks."

"Jayce, I'm sorry."

"Nice try," Jayce says coldly.

He picks up a cloth pouch and stands up, but misses his belt when he tries to slide it in. As he tries to catch it, the tie on the pouch opens and something inside glows a bluish-purple color.

Tash catches the pouch and looks inside. He is careful not to touch it. "This is a black magic gem. Where did you get it?"

Jayce snatches it back and tucks the pouch into a pocket in his belt.

Tash blocks his way out. "Those are dangerous."

"So is betrayal." Jayce says seriously.

Tash notices Lord Darkshadow's journal in the open trunk. "I thought you got rid of that?"

Jayce chuckles sarcastically. "Why, because you told

me to?" He shakes his head and walks toward the door.

Tash grabs him by the arm. Jayce stares at Tash with a dark strength that Tash hasn't seen in him before. Jayce's glare moves to his grip as a threat to let him go.

"You know I didn't betray you," Tash says firmly. "Chloe isn't ready. If she tries now, she'll fail."

"And whose fault is that? You were supposed to train her."

"We just need more time."

Jayce walks out.

"What are you going to do?"

He catches up to Jayce with such urgency that boys look up from what they are doing, alarmed. Jayce calms down, hiding his anger to protect the boys. Their faith in him and in Tash and the prophecy, had kept them together as a team. Without that hope, it would be chaos.

Jayce grabs Tash in a headlock grinning like he is teasing, but squeezing a little too hard. Tash smiles and makes a playful choking sound.

"OK. I give," he squeaks.

Jayce drops him in the dirt and walks off briskly. The boys think Jayce and Tash are goofing around and go back about their business. Tash catches up to him.

"Wait. Whatever your plan is, let me do it," Tash offers quietly.

"You've never been down there. You wouldn't make it past the dragon guard."

A boy opens the hidden door as Jayce reaches it.

Tash stops just inside. "I'll figure something out then. Today. Please, wait. Stay here where it's safe."

"Safe?" Jayce stares at him, astonished. "Go back to your fairyland, Tashuhunka."

Jayce disappears inside his shadow and slips out.

Outside, in the main ravine of the mines, Jayce moves his shadow among the crevices in the jagged terrain, slips past a guard troll and makes his way to the train level. The small engine, pulling six ore cars of fairydust, bolts toward him on rickety tracks. Jayce clings to the side of one of the cars and moves with the shadows hiding from dragon guards. Fairydust blows onto his hand making it visible just as he passes by the guard station. He moves his hand just in time then blows the dust from it quickly. A guard does a double take, but doesn't see him.

Hidden in his shadow, Jayce jumps off and creeps around the feet of the guards. One of the guards steps on him and knocks into the guard next to him.

"Hey!" The guard shoves the other one back.

Jayce dives into a somersault. It looks like flickering light as he rolls behind storage bins outside of Cosentino's quarters. When the coast is clear he sneaks inside.

Cosentino's bedroom is luxurious. The overstuffed troll is sleeping on a feather bed under a velvet canopy still in his work clothes, as if he fell asleep the moment he laid down. He snores so loudly that at first Jayce thinks something is wrong with him. Jayce steps out of his shadow, appearing in the room. The irony of the extravagence in this prison makes Jayce grin.

"Cosentino, you have the taste of a gentleman," he says under his breath.

Cosentino stirs in his lavish bedding.

"And you're seriously into cushy velvet pillows," Jayce touches one, then feels its satin tassel. A half-eaten cheese log with nut sauce is arranged on a dainty china plate on an elegantly carved table. Jayce takes Cosentino's blade from the cheese.

Jayce moves next to the troll and presses the knife to his throat while holding a gem in his other hand.

"You do have a way out of here," he says softly.

Cosentino wakes up angry, but the gem shining with blue ultraviolet light catches his eye. "A black jewel? They do exist." He is ecstatic as he reaches for it.

"Not so fast," Jayce says pulling it away. "If you want these, they come with a price."

"Of course. Where did you find it?" Cosentino sits up, wide awake and more interested in the gem than what Jayce is doing in his quarters.

"A bargain. Our freedom for the vein," Jayce barters.

"For you and me both," Cosentino lets out a roaring laugh. "I'd like to get out of here as much as you."

"Gee, why don't I believe you?" Jayce says, stabbing a piece of cheese. Cosentino grabs the knife from him.

"Not everything is as it seems. Especially down here."

"Right," Jayce knows better than to argue. "Well, tell me then. When we make quota, what does the witch have planned for us? The truth this time."

"You don't want to know," Cosentino says chewing the chunk of nutty Edam cheese. The troll may have the taste of a gentlemen but he does not eat like one. It is disgusting. But, not even the slimy nuts dripping from the warts on Cosentino's chin can deter Jayce from his goal.

"How about you set us free instead?" He looks the slob right in the eyes.

"You want cupcakes and balloons too? Cosentino sneers.

"I'm serious," Jayce tells him.

"It's out of my control. The minute you make quota, three quarters of ya are lunch meat." Cosentino pops the remainder of the cheese log in his mouth.

"And the rest?" Jayce already suspects but wants to know it all. He is still trying to figure a way for all of his men to survive.

"She gets a kick outta you troublemakers. The hag will probably turn you into something' and keep ya around for laughs."

Cosentino wipes the drool from his face and winks at Jayce.

"If she likes troublemakers, maybe she'll make a deal with a snitch." Jayce knew better, but said it anyway.

Cosentino back-hands him across the room. Jayce is ready for it. He flips and lands on his feet.

"Do not threaten me boy," Cosentino growls. He takes off his shirt and tosses it into a laundry basket.

"You give me no choice," Jayce replies defiantly.

"The scanner is on a direct feed to the hag." Cosentino powders his hairy armpits and picks up a clean shirt. The irony is almost too much for Jayce.

"Even if I wanted to get you out," Cosentino goes on, "there's no way to load all you guys on the trains between counts."

"So the trains DO go farther than the castle. What? They make it past the force field? Under it?"

"Air's pure poison. Even us trolls need gear."

"You want the gems, work it out." He tosses Cosentino the gem. The troll holds it up to the light mystified by it. Jayce is about to exit when he hears LB calling him through his earpiece.

"An extra body showed up on the count. They found Tash," LB said frantically. "Dragons are chasing him up the secret tunnel."

Cosentino gets a call at the same time. His expression changes immediately. He picks Jayce up and throws him against the wall so hard he crashes through it. Jayce lands on the control deck knocking two Oddizen guards flat on their faces. Cosentino charges after him. Jayce trips Cosentino off his feet with a sweeping kick. He falls so hard rocks shook out of the cavern wall.

Guards try to grab Jayce, but he fights them off easily. Taking the cue, the other boys fight their guards and within moments, the skirmish has escalated in to a full-grown riot.

Strongarm and Wiggins land in a flying pedal car, powered by three boys. Strongarm throws a net over Jayce's head but Jayce flips out of it. Strongarm grabs Jayce by the back of the neck. Jayce spins upward in a roundhouse kick, and cuts Strongarm with the edge of his boot. He somersaults backwards out of his grasp while Wiggins just flaps nervously next to them.

Cosentino grabs Max by the neck, choking him.

"All right. All RIGHT. You win." Jayce gives himself up.

The guards converge on him. Strongarm kicks Jayce hard in the back, knocking him to the ground. The other boys surrender. Cosentino lets Max go and picks Jayce up by the back of the neck.

"I should have known better than to do an honest deal with you." Jayce huffed. He is still trying to negotiate.

"I told ya not to threaten me." Cosentino pushes his way through a crowd of salivating trolls and Oddizens to the edge of the cliff. Jayce digs his heels into the dirt, trying to stop but it is no use. Cosentino has him teetering on his toes. "I gotta make an example of you now," Cosentino is angry about it.

Below them, the large-mouthed lizard-like creature stomps anxiously through the lava river unharmed, then stops and waits directly under Jayce.

"I can think of so many other ways," Jayce says, struggling nervously.

The crowd pushes against them and the ledge begins to crack under Cosentino's feet. Jayce clings to his hairy arms trying desperately not to fall. Cosentino pulls him back. The troll respects Jayce, or at least enjoys fighting with him.

"You want me to kill someone else instead? I'm good with that. Pick one," he says.

"No."

How can Jayce choose someone else to die? He stops struggling and looks at the creature below, ready to succumb to becoming its lunch. Just then, LB yells across the ravine.

"Cosentino! Let him go!"

Cosentino breaks out in a full belly laugh at the sight of the youngest boy shouting orders at him. LB pushes on a lever, tilting carloads of gemstones toward the lava river.

"No!" Cosentino is so upset he choked on his yell.

"Let him go," LB says it slower this time.

Cosentino grumbles and then shoves Jayce into a cage on a chain. He glares at Jayce as he shuts and locks the door. "Now you can watch 'em all die before you," he says harshly.

Cosentino turns back to LB as Strongarm hoists the cage up to the top of the cavern. "OK. You work, he lives. Now put my gems down. Carefully," Cosentino growls angrily.

LB lets go of the lever and the carts were leveled back on the tracks. Armed guards converge on him.

"I know. I know," LB puts his hands up. This is a familiar routine.

Jayce watches from above as LB and several other boys are pushed down a well-worn path to a small arena with a thick wooden post at the center. He closes his eyes, dreading what is coming next. The splintered post is dented and stained with blood from the fists of all the boys forced to punch it over the years—for the slightest infractions. The guards are always careful, making them hit it enough to hurt but still able to work in the mines.

In the beginning it was a game for the guards. They bet the number of punches each boy could last through. The boys were given an out. If a boy revealed the name of the heir, he would be freed. No one ever did, though. Even IF any of them had known who the heir was, rule under Hagla would have been devastating for the world. They were determined to protect their families and as long as the witch thought the heir might be among them, they were of value to her. But after years of defiant silence, the guards stopped asking about the heir and the game became sadistic punishment.

An Oddizen guard flicks his knotted whip over LB's head, signaling him to begin. LB hits the post with such anger, the flesh on his knuckles splits open on the first punch. The guards roar wildly.

"Chloe's not coming is she?" he whispers through his communicator to Jayce.

"No," Jayce says softly.

LB was hoping for a different answer.

"We're screwed," he huffs, hitting the post again.

"Yeah. Pretty much." Jayce sits back in his cage. A flood of emotion comes over him and tears of frustration well up in his eyes. He has failed.

CHAPTER 5

Tash swerves hard, narrowly missing the pointed tip of a stalactite as he flies up the secret tunnel with the Black Dragon and Icky hot on his tail. The last section of the tunnel is narrow and straight up, and the dragons were fast. Their flames are closing in on him. He spins around and shoots an arrow into chard of rocks. The rocks fall, blocking the path, but the Black Dragon breaks through in seconds.

Tash looks back at the wrong moment and grazes the wall, knocking his arrows onto the rocks. The dragons are nearly upon him. Tash takes a chance and grabs one, then hightails it upward, scanning the rocky surfaces for the right place to take his last shot. He spots a crack in the ceiling just before the end of the tunnel and spins his arrow into it. The loosened rocks fall distracting the dragons. They fly out the tunnel and slam right into the force field.

SMACK! It shocks them unconscious and they fall backwards into a carefully positioned cage where a spring-loaded lid snaps down, locking them inside.

Tash ducks behind bushes and crawls through a hole he had camouflaged and rigged with magnets to create an opening in the force field. His heart is pounding in his chest as he climbs out on the other side. He has never come that close to being caught before–and now that the dragons found his tunnel it will be too dangerous to go back in. His mind is racing. He takes cover in a tree next to Mrs. B's Bakery on Penstemon's Main Street and catches his breath.

Mrs. B's Bakery is bustling with the morning rush, anxious for their decaf latte, green tea or hot cocoa fix. Mrs. B gave me a job, shortly after I moved in with Tip. I had shifts before and after school and some Saturdays. She needed the help, and I wanted to work. It's a good fit and I like her. It doesn't pay much, but it is pretty easy normally and Mrs. B gives me baked goods for the house. Pops says I don't have to, but I like to contribute.

I've been feeling odd lately and I'm not getting much sleep. I've been having nightmares and dreams–mostly about that beautiful guy, and other boys–but there aren't any boys my age in Penstemon. I don't know what's going on, but there is no way I am going to tell Tash about it. We haven't spoken for...well, a long time. He is always around–everywhere I go. But he doesn't talk to me. He just hides and watches me. It is kind of spooky honestly...and sad. I don't know what I did to make him so mad at me, but whatever it is I wish I could take it back.

I guess I am lost in my thoughts because when the crowd at the counter parts for Monica, I hit myself in the face with the steamer.

Monica hates me. She is the prissy queen-wannabe leader of the elite Periwinkle Fairy clique. A group that I have absolutely no interest in. Their idea of excitement is shopping online while watching fashion videos. Not that it's a bad thing, it's just not for me, or my wallet.

"Here you go, Priscilla." As I pass a latte to her, I see that guy in a reflection of the stainless steel pitcher. *Is he here?* I look around and behind me.

"I am over here, Chloe." Monica says. Her sneer is always so heartwarming. "Priscilla, hold this." She passes her a tabloid with a paparazzi photo of Prince Peter on the cover. Priscilla takes it with glee. Monica continues, "I will have a non-fat mocha hazelnut Brazilian cocoa latte with a sprinkle of nutmeg, a swirl of Amaretto almond whipped cream, oh and a fairyberry cinnamon bagel and make it snappy, will you? Please." She says it as fast as she can, trying to slip me up.

"Sure." Come on, this is a bakery, not rocket science. The minute my back is turned, Monica dumps my backpack out on the counter.

"Ooooh! Look at this!" she squeals. She holds up my photo album between her fingernails like it has cooties. "So sweet, Pillywiggin. Love the stenciled hearts and flowers," she whines wickedly.

"Give it back, Monica."

"Why is it still empty, Chloe? Oh that's right. You have no family." Monica drops the album with the money for her latte and leaves with the other fairies twittering in high-pitched chirps behind her. She turns around at the door to toss one last word at me, "Orphan."

Mrs. B helps me gather my stuff. My glasses must be fogged up from the steam.

"Chloe, pay no attention to Monica. She's envious. You are loved by everyone, especially me." Mrs. B always knows the perfect thing to say.

"I know today is especially difficult for you, sweetheart, your birthday's usually are."

"You think today is my birthday?" That surprises me.

"You have mood swings about this time every year, dear."

Now she is sounding like Tip. But it makes sense.

"This year has been the weirdest. I am seeing things, and hearing things."

"Perhaps you should take some time off. Get some rest, dear."

"Yes, maybe. Mrs. B, I've been wondering...what happened to all the boys?"

Mrs. B's expression suddenly goes blank. "What did you say, dear?"

"Why aren't there any boys in our town?"

It was like she didn't hear me. Really strange. I hear someone CRYING, but no one else is in the room.

"Did you hear that?"

"I'm not sure." Mrs. B says with wide-eyes, trying hard to understand.

"Boys. B O Y S... here, like Peter." Everyone knows who Peter is.

"Oh yes," she says with relief, "Why are you suddenly interested in Prince Peter?"

"I'm not, I just wondered why there aren't any boys my age here?"

She stares at me so blankly I wonder if I said it right. I am about done with this line of questioning. Then she perks up.

"Prince Peter is visiting from boarding school. He should be at the extravaganza today."

"Extravaganza! I'm late," I realize. "I was supposed to meet Tip and Darling ten minutes ago."

CHAPTER 6

The Annual Penstemon Extravaganza and Water Gala is THE event the whole town looks forward to every year. Arriving fashionably on time, King Kenneth and Queen Rose park their convertible 1957 pink Cadillac behind the concession stand. The king has a thing for junk food. The queen never touches it. King Ken and the fast food manager have their routine of sneaking a snack past the queen down to a science. Of course, she is on to them, but she lets the king have his fun. The royals are a strange match. She is lovely, regal and refined and he is...approachable–like the guy-next-door-kind-of-approachable–not like a "king" at all. He was also a third of her size, not that it matters. You can tell that they care for each other. He makes her laugh, she is sweet to him. But something seems "off" about them.

As Prince Peter steps out of the car to follow his parents, I make a beeline to the other side of the pond, where Tip and Darling are supposed to be waiting for me. But, since I am late, they started. The plan is to help Darling learn to fly. Her body hasn't matured yet and her wings are, well, small.

She rides a dragonfly named Appleton normally, but she decided to go on her own today. She is standing on the water with two large leaves strapped to her feet. Tip is trying, but failing, to steady her. I grab her other arm and pull her up just before Darling does the splits.

"Darling, are you sure about this?"

"I have ridden Appleton long enough. Today, I will fly on my own, right past the amazed crowd on the beach to ooo's and aahs and applause." Darling may be small but she is feisty.

Tip and I hold Darling's arms and push her as she flaps her wings hard, trying to get lift off.

"Maybe this isn't a good idea," Darling says wobbling.

"Nonsense. It's a perfect way to learn how to fly." Tip likes to finish things.

"Flap harder," I tell her. I look down and see a that guy in a reflection, floating on the surface of the water. He is sitting with his head down and it feels like he is sad. Really sad. Devastated.

"Who is that?"

"What are you talking about?" Tip looks but only sees the Periwinkle Fairies, just up ahead. They are in a seven fairy water-ski pyramid formation with Monica on top. "Let's slow down a bit."

The loud popping of fuchsia buds starts the gala, triggering streams of ribbons and flower petals that flutter over the glimmering sunlit pond.

"This is it," Monica gleams. "We do this right and

we'll be dining at the palace tonight, with the prince!"

Fairybabies on parade sprinkle rose petals over Monica and her waterskiing fairy pyramid as they pass the beach Monica has slapped on so much lip gloss that the reflection of the sun on her smile blinds the first three rows.

It's so funny it makes me forget what I am doing. We are going too fast. Darling is trying to stay upright with Tip and I holding her by her armpits.

Something flickers on the horizon. I can't take my eyes off it. It is a thin blur, shaped like one of those stealth bombers, almost invisible but growing darker as it glides silently toward me. I close and open my eyes, but it keeps coming. It's HIM, glaring, like he can see me. I try to avoid him but he sweeps right through me. The anger is so intense I feel like I am going to throw up.

"Chloe! What are you doing? You're going to knock us into the lake."

"I thought he was going to crash into us." I look behind me, but he has disappeared. Maybe he was never there at all.

"He?"

"I'm losing it. I'm seeing boys everywhere."

"Do you have a thing for Prince Peter? Is that why you've been blushing all week? Tip laughs. "You're delusional. You don't even know him."

"Must be hormones." Darling huffs breathlessly.

"Do fairies get hormones?" My glasses are falling off my nose but I don't want to let go and drop Darling.

"Tilt your head back," Tip says.

"I can't look where I'm going that way."

"Use your peripheral." Tip loves using large words. "Look straight ahead and peek out the sides."

I did.

"It is really hard to see this way."

I shake my head trying to work my glasses back into position. Tip laughs at me.

"Glad to be so amusing."

"Guys!" Darling gasps with horror.

What? I start to say, but the horror of what is about to happen stops the word from coming out. We lose our grip and Darling plows right into Monica and her fairy pyramid jettisoning them out of control into nearby trees. Fairybabies scream with glee and buzz the crowd. Monica ends up dangling upside-down over the royal box by the bottom of her bathing suit that is caught in a tree. She is so mad she is quiet.

Prince Peter howls with laughter.

"Oh, those poor girls," Queen Rose says attempting not to laugh. "They must be so embarrassed." She succumbs and giggles in the most elegant way.

"It's funny," Peter laughs. "And I thought this was going to be dull."

Monica is so angry her eyes bulge as she glares at us.

"Okay, time to go."

Appleton catches Darling on his back and the next thing I know we are on the other side of the pond–or at least what used to be the pond.

"What happened to the water?"

"They dammed up the pond to make the Pentsemon side deeper for the water show," Tip explains.

I hear the crying sound coming from beneath the dry lake bed.

"Can you hear that?" I didn't wait for their answer, I darted right toward the sound. "Here, behind this rock. Help me push it aside."

Tip and Darling look confused but help anyway. There is a large root hole behind the rock. I can hear the crying louder now. I don't hesitate. I run inside and fall straight down. The tunnel twists downward, widening at the bottom. I land on a ledge. It was suddenly pretty scary. The only light comes from a glow about a hundred feet down. Tip lands next to me, while Darling hovers on Appleton.

"It's too hot. Appleton's wings are getting crispy," Darling complains.

"Chloe, this is the Mantlerealm. We're not supposed to be in here. It's dangerous."

A hairy spider falls on Tip's shoulder, making her jump. Fortunately for the spider, it scurries away.

I hear the crying echoing off the cavern walls. It is like it is calling to me. I have to go forward. I drop farther down onto another ledge, where there is some kind of animal path.

Turning the corner, I find myself face to giant nostril of Zenuvius who is asleep on the path. My body tiptoes backwards. "Okay, I see your point."

Tip peaks around the corner and freezes. I shut her

dropped jaw with one finger.

"A...a DRAGON?" She freaks out, very quietly.

The crying is louder now.

"You guys go back. I've got to do this." I tell them.

"Do what?" Darling asks.

"Save someone, I think. I know it sounds ridiculous, but I feel like something inside is telling me to follow the crying." I point to a tunnel on the far side of the ravine. "It's coming from over there."

"You mean like little voices?" Darling asks with beady eyes.

"She's totally lost it. She's been dreaming, or should I say, delusional, all week," Tip huffs impatiently.

By the time Tip finishes her sentence, Darling has made it past Zenuvius with Appleton in hand. Tip sighs, then takes her turn. She watches Zenuvius take a breath, then tip-toes under his nose to catch up to Darling.

I freeze mid-way. My mind goes blank. I am standing face to eyeball with a very large sleeping dragon. All I can think of is he has the biggest nostrils I've ever seen.

"Chloe." She gives me the "look". Then she and Darling high-tail it for the other tunnel.

Zenuvius' eyelids flutter and he starts to exhale. *Okay, this is not good.* I am thinking to myself. He opens one eye. *Why am I pausing? Go, GO, GOOOO!*

Zenuvius whips his tail so hard he splits a boulder as he speeds after me. His dragonshrill echoes loudly, shaking the walls. He blows flames at my toes. *Ow, ow, ow, OW.*

I duck into the tunnel after Tip and Darling.

Zenuvius slams into the tunnel nose-first.

"He can't fit! Yay."

"He's stuck," Darling deadpans.

He beats his nose side-to-side, but the rocks hold firm. He huffs and inhales angrily.

"Uh, guys..." Tip whispers as she grabs our hands and backs away.

"It's okay. He can't open his mouth wide enough," I say with relief.

He blows a plume of fire not even large enough to toast a marshmellow.

"Whew."

We head toward light that is shining from a cavern in front of us. But this time, we are more careful.

CHAPTER 7

I reach the other side of the tunnel first, but pause this time, before looking out. I lay down, like Tash taught me, and peek carefully around the edge.

Pint-sized spotted creatures are busily breaking surface rock from gemstones with tiny hammers inside a steaming cave. A river of lava winds around boulders, flowing into a tunnel on the other side.

Tip, Darling and Appleton, stack on top of me and poke their heads out to see.

"What are those?" Darling whispers.

"Oddizens. Wow, they're more gruesome-looking than their pictures in the *Encyclopedia of Mystical Creatures*." Tip turns our dangerous mission into an educational excursion.

"They don't see us," I realize, standing up. None of the creatures notice me. Tip, Darling and Appleton join me as I walk further into the cavern. I step right next to one and it doesn't look up.

"Guys, think about it. What could be so important that it would be guarded by a fire-breathing dragon and THEM?"

"I wouldn't say guarded," Tip quips.

A glimmer of something catches my eye. There is plume of billowing steam coming from a circle of rocks in the lava river. We fly to it.

"Ugh, it's so hot. My wings hurt, Tip says.

I see a birdcage inside the steam.

"It's wood. How can a wooden birdcage not burn up, here?" I wonder outloud. "Someone's in it!"

I reach out to touch it. Tip yanks my arm back.

"Wait. Chloe. Do you realize that the only person who could have worked a spell here is Hagla, as in the wicked witch of the Heatherworld?" Tip whispers with wide eyes.

A figure inside the cage stands up. The gentle flutter of its wings moves the steam enough to partially see it.

"It's a FAIRY," Darling gasps with astonishment.

"She must have been calling to me," I sigh.

Tip perks up. "Only a handful of fairies can speak telepathically."

"Do you think she's my mother?" She is looking right at me but is surprised when I speak. "We'll get you out, don't worry."

Darling kicks a rock over the steam vent. When the air clears, Appleton gasps. He knows her.

"Judith," he says faintly, absolutely shocked.

She is misty from the steam and very beautiful.

"Good fairy?" Darling asks.

"Very good fairy," Appleton smiles.

Tip examines the cage. "There's no door," she says frantically.

"Tip, help me unhook the chain. I have a plan." I have an unnerving sense that the mood of the Oddizens is shifting. I feel like we should hurry. "Darling, you guys take the other end. Secure your feet against those rocks. We'll dip the bottom of the cage into the lava river and burn it off."

"Burn it...?" Tip has that wide-eyed look again.

"Do you have a better idea? I actually hope you do."

"Nope."

"Darling?" She shakes her head no.

Appleton shrugs. "There will be no fairy fondue today, let's follow Chloe's lead. Everyone grab hold tightly."

Judith clings to the inside top of the cage. Everyone gets into position. Tip and I unhitch the heavy chain from its pulley. The pulley hits the lava river and disintegrates before it sinks.

"That's not good," Darling huffs.

A blast of hot air singes our wings as we lower the bottom of the cage into the flowing mantle.

"The current is too strong. I'm losing it," Tip exclaims frantically.

The chain is tugged out of her hands. I can't hold it up by myself. The bottom of the cage touches the lava and burns off instantly. Tip catches the end of the chain just in time. As soon as we pull up, the cage catches fire. Judith flies out and we drop it.

The Oddizens all look up, and notice us.

"Time to go!" Tip sings.

Judith opens her arms and extends her luminous wings.

"Quick, gather around me." She wraps her wings around all of us.

The Oddizens lunge at us, drooling and chomping their sharp, jagged teeth. I feel a knobby tongue and slimy lips on my neck when we disappear in a FLASH of brilliant white light.

I am still slapping at the thing that was about to eat me when we rematerialize by the pond in the Penstemon forest.

Whew. I drop to my knees to wash the drool off my neck.

Tip bobs up and down frantic-like. She always does that when she is nervous. "That was way too close," Tip gasps.

"Well, at least we found out I wasn't going insane."

"Jury's still out on that." Tip is only half-teasing.

Judith is mesmerizing. She moves with such grace. She is everything you envision a fairy to look like. Her long hair sparkles in the sunlight as she kneels by the pond and fills her hands with water to take a long, satisfying drink. She looks like a truly magical being.

"We teleported," Tip realizes. "How can you do magic without fairydust?"

"True power comes from within," Judith explains calmly. She is even more enchanting smiling. "But that was the last of mine for awhile." She gazes around the forest relishing everything.

"What was with those Oddizens? I mean were they weird or what?" Darling is still shuddering.

"Hagla thought I would talk them into letting me go, so she cast a spell focusing them on the gems. When the cage broke, so did the spell." Judith suddenly seems anxious.

I offer a handshake. "I'm Chloe. This is Tip, Darling and Appleton."

"My name is Judith," she smiles, definitely distracted. "We haven't met have we? You look familiar."

"Judith as in Supreme Fairy and Guardian of the Light, Judith?" Tip asks.

"That's me," she answers. "Although I haven't been guardian of much since Hagla tricked me into that birdcage. Thank you for rescuing me. How did you get into the mantlerealm?"

"A roothole in the bottom of the pond," Tip says perkily.

"They dammed up the pond for the water extravaganza," Darling adds, "So the Bladderwhack side was dried up."

"Oh dear," Judith says worriedly. "That means they can get out. Will you show me?"

"Sure, the dam's right over here."

Standing at the bottom of the dam, Judith sizes up the rocks to find one that would open the water flow at the bottom. Together, we use a log as a lever to knock it loose. Water leaks through slowly. After a moment, it flows faster.

"Should we plug the roothole?" I ask.

Judith gasps in such a high tone it sounds like she squeaked. "Yes! Hurry!"

We move the rock back over the roothole just before the pond water reaches us. We fly out of the way and land on the grassy shore.

"I hope Monica isn't doing her show again," Darling grins slyly.

"Do you want to find out?" Tip asks.

"No."

Judith seems relieved.

"Why did we just do that?" I ask Judith.

She pauses, then starts to explain.

A fly buzzes around my head and I accidentally knocking my glasses off, shooing it away.

"Why did Hagla imprison you?" Tip may not have heard my question, or her curiosity got the best of her, but Judith's answer is off the wall.

"Hagla has really bad hair. She's always been jealous. Poor thing, teased as a child. She hung me over a steam vent so my hair would frizz. Ha! Backfire! It turned my hair gel into a fabulous conditioner. And have you ever seen tinier pores in your life?"

"Uh..." Tip cannot think of a response.

"You didn't hear a word I said." Judith recognizes our dumbfounded looks, I guess.

"We heard you." Darling says wide-eyed, desperately trying not to make an expression that might insult Judith.

It's just like my conversation with Mrs. B. "Must be a communication spell."

Everyone looks at me really funny. I don't want to know what they heard me say. I change the subject.

"Do you have children, Judith?"

"No, why?"

I put my glasses back on and hide my disappointment. "I was just thinking that they'd be happy to see you again. That is, if you had any."

Judith smiles at me. "Sweet. Is Queen Rose still at the palace? I am certain that the Queen will reward you for your bravery."

"Oh, I would love to meet her," Darling says excitedly.

"You guys go ahead." I say grinning.

I head deeper into the forest. Tip calls after me, but I pretend I don't hear her. She and Darling will have a great time returning Judith to the palace and meeting the King and Queen, and Peter. I'm not up to a celebration right now. I had really hoped that Judith was my mother.

CHAPTER 8

The sun hangs low on the horizon reflecting a rainbow of colors in nimbus clouds that are scattered through the twilight-blue sky. I am upset, and not thinking, and because of that, I am oblivious to a giant brown owl until it nearly catches me.

SCREEECH!

Okay, I am awake now! I dart for the floor of the forest. The owl is fast. It chases me around trees as if it knows what I am thinking and which way I am going to turn. I feel its breath on my foot as it tries to grab my toes with its beak.

I duck down. Too fast. I almost lose it. I spin the other way. My heart is beating so hard I can't hear anything else.

SQUAAAAAWK!

Silence.

I turn to look behind me. *Tash? Did he snare the owl?*

I smack the side of my face into a tree.

Suddenly, it is dark and I am gagging. Something has hold of my feet. I freak out. I kick and struggle to get away but their grasp is strong. I am pulled up from the darkness. The suction is so strong, I almost lose my glasses. I hold onto them as I am jerked upward. I land in something wet and gooey. I really don't want to look. My glasses are still on my face but covered in mud. I take them off and see what I am sitting up to my waist in.

"Bladderwhack sludge, ugh."

This is where run off from the garlic beds ends up on the far side of the pond. I am covered in it, head to toe, except for two clean circles around my eyes. Lovely.

"Are you okay?" Tash offers his hand to help me stand up.

I haven't seen him up this close in a really long time. Actually, who can see? I reach for his blurry shape. When we touch, it feels like time stops.

"Tash?"

I stand up, squinting, two inches away from his face, my lip curled up in a sneer and mud dripping from my hair onto my cheek. I can finally see him clearly. I am so focused on his gentle welcoming hands, graceful strong arms, muscular bare chest, shiny black hair and handsome, brown eyes, that the sucking sound of my bum dislodging from the stinky gunk is hardly noticeable. I don't notice my feet hurt until I stand fully on them.

"Ow."

"I'm sorry. Did I hurt you?" He says with such sincere concern it warms my heart.

"No, Dragonfire. Singed my toes."

His alarmed reaction shoots me back to reality.

"Where did you see a dragon?"

"You don't know? I thought you were always watching me. What kind of stalker are you?"

Tash straightens up, taking offense.

"I'm kidding. It was a joke."

He used to have a sense of humor.

"I would to hug you but," I motion at the foul-smelling sludge I am covered in.

"Please don't." He says seriously. He is stoic, even for Tash.

I give him my best smile. "Thank you for snaring that owl."

"You know better than to fly after sunset. You weren't even paying attention," he scolds.

"I have a lot on my mind."

"Since when?" he glares at me.

Harsh.

"Okay, now that we've insulted each other, can we stop? This is the first conversation we've had in a really long time."

Something is up with him.

"What's the matter?" I ask.

He steps back, like he is uncomfortable being so close to me. His expression finally softens and he looks at me, up and down. For a moment, I think it is nice, like maybe he likes what he sees...but nope, he is just checking for wounds.

"If you're all right I should go," he says.

"Can't you stay? I miss you. You're just gonna go sit in a tree. Sit here. You never talk to me anymore."

"I talk." He says defensively.

"Heckling doesn't count." Okay, that gets a smile. He even looks at me affectionately. I feel myself blushing and am embarrassed-like he can see red cheeks under the mud, but still, I look down.

He almost holds me, but stops himself.

"Tash we used to be best friends. What happened?" Before I finish my sentence, he is gone. I sigh my hurt feelings out, "now you can't wait to get away."

I dive into the clear water of the pond and wash the sludge off. I wash my glasses off and look for him, but don't see him.

—▸≻◆≺◂——≪◆▣◆≫——▸≻◆≺◂——≪◆▣◆≫——▸≻◆≺◂——≪◆▣◆≫——▸≻◆≺◂—

Tash hides in a nearby pine tree, camoflaged in its shadows. From his view, the sunset, mirrored in the surface of the pond shimmers as he watches Chloe flying upward and shaking wet glistening droplets from her clean body and hair. He has such feelings for her that he sees her slow motion, spiraling in a rainbow of sunlight toward sparkling stars in a darkening sky.

—▸≻◆≺◂——≪◆▣◆≫——▸≻◆≺◂——≪◆▣◆≫——▸≻◆≺◂——≪◆▣◆≫——▸≻◆≺◂—

I know I am going to get an earful when I arrive home home after dark, if Tip beats me home. I am hoping she is still at the Palace, so I fly fast, but more carefully this time.

Our tiny village called Bladderwhack is a cozy nestling of pieced together environmentally-friendly dwellings. The village is supposed to be named Bladderack after a yellow flower with a black center that grows along the shore of the pond here. But the guy reading the job order had a big wad of gum in his mouth when he told his buddy what to paint on the sign. When they realized the mistake, rather than repainting the sign, they decided to rename the village. Not many people ever come to Bladderwhack on purpose anyway.

Pops is waiting for me in the doorway of our trailer. Thunderbunny pounces on me as I limp up. He is my brother, sort of. I mean, I grew up with a litter of bunnies and of all of them he and I are the closest. He is odd too. His feet and ears are so enormous for his small body that when he twirls he gets lift off, like a helicopter.

Tip steps from behind Pops. She is angry. Arms crossed and foot tapping. "It's past dark," she snips.

"I'm sorry to worry you." I had never been out so late before. I grin nervously at Pops.

"Where'd you get the shiner?" Thunderbunny asks, covering his nose.

"I have a black eye?" *Wonderful,* I thought.

Thunderbunny's cheeks puff out and he holds his breath.

"I fell in the Bladderwhack sludge,"I explain.

"Yeah, we figured that out," he deadpans.

"A bag of frozen peas on that eye and the swelling should go down in a couple of weeks." Pops grins at me teasingly, then, hustles to the kitchen.

Thunderbunny and Tip follow me into the bedroom. Thunderbunny opens a window while Tip turns on the bath. She pours a whole bottle of flower oil and half a bottle of bubble bath in the hot water.

"I don't smell that bad...do I?"

They are too polite to say.

"Okay, maybe I do."

"What's with you lately? You could have been eaten by an owl. Or worse." Tip says it with more shrill than usual.

"What's worse than being eaten by an owl?"

I don't think Thunderbunny really wants to know.

Tip doesn't answer anyway.

The events of the day sweep over me like a tidal wave of emotion, sucking the energy right out of me. I sit down.

"I thought she was my mother. I hoped anyway. I'm never going to find my family."

"Your family? What are we?" Tip snoots.

"You're right. I'm sorry." I don't normally cry. Now I can't stop. The more I try, the more tears come out.

"What? Now waterworks?"

Tip says it so seriously it makes me laugh. Then she laughs. My next laugh came out as a snort.

"Holy moly," she rolls her eyes at me.

Thunderbunny breaks into the song, "Don't Worry, Be Happy." He has a low voice like James Earl Jones and moves like a dancer. Always cheers me up.

Little did we know that an owl was watching us from a tree outside our window.

CHAPTER 9

A spotted gray owl peers into Chloe's bedroom window watching the happy scene. Thunderbunny belts a big one just as the viewpoint zooms from their bedroom window up through the eyes of the owl and out to the floating surface of the witch's black cauldron.

"OH, PLEASE! Somebody GAG the RABBIT!" Hagla belches.

Owls are spies for the evil witch. She views the world outside her electromagnetic prison through their eyes in the liquid magic of her portable stew pot.

She gawks at Thunderbunny with sinister delight as she stands at a table piled with books, potions, contorted dead creatures and her cauldron in the center. Tabloid magazines are neatly displayed on a coffee table next to an elaborate Gothic fireplace. Her laboratory is decorated in a mix of ancient Goth and European furnishings complete with a leopard print sofa and red velvet curtains that frame tall open windows on two sides of the room.

Hagla wails with displeasure when the view in the

cauldron flips upside-down and Tash's face comes into view. It seems like he is staring at her. The cauldron's image turns black as the connection to the owl is disrupted. Hagla throws a glass bottle against the wall scaring her scrawny cat, Snickets.

"RREEEEOW!" Snickets screeches, jumping claws out, ten feet in the air.

"Mr. Snivels! Mr. Snivels!" Hagla screams.

Mr. Snivels runs in huffing with Wiggins, who has a bandage on his waist from this morning.

"When are you going to capture that boy?" She screeches furiously.

"Tashuhunka is very clever, mistress." Mr. Snivels says politely with his Scottish accent.

Zenuvius limps in with two black eyes and a scratched nose, steaming mad. "He's not the one you should worry about," he huffs.

"Zenuvius! What happened?" Hagla's tone changes to maternal.

"Fairies," he mumbles, embarrassed that they got away from him.

"Hmm?"

"Perhaps I can explain, mistress," Mr. Snivels has a way with her. He waves Zenuvius off to calm down then looks up kindly at the witch.

Hagla blushes and primps herself in a mirror.

"Please stop calling me mistress. It makes me sound like a wanton woman," she coos, batting her eyes at Mr. Snivels. "Although that's not entirely a bad thing."

Wiggins can't take it. "Honey, forget it. That "do" is a lost cause. I mean it looks like it needs a permit. A dog tag. Like it died and you're too attached to throw it out." He looks around, straightening an imaginary tie—a bit he copied from a great, old, dead comedian. "Am I the only one who sees the humor in it? I mean, come on. It's killin' me."

Hagla slithers toward him sinisterly like a snake. "You are new?" She says sweetly.

Mr. Snivels quickly backs away from Wiggins.

"Yes. Nice of you to notice," he says proudly. "I'm just takin' the gig as a fill in job while I look for a new agent. Snivels said you wouldn't mind. Always in need of help, he said."

Wiggins stands taller, basking in the attention then, he whisks out a long list that unfolds like a scroll.

"I have a few suggestions, to liven things up, if you're into it."

The expression on her face tells him that he has just overstepped the employee-boss relationship. Hagla is NOT pleased. Wiggins gulps and rolls the scroll back up. Then he takes a note from his vest pocket.

Mr. Snivels takes another step away from him.

"Oh yeah. The reason I'm here. Uh, I'm supposed to tell ya," he reads the note again. "Some broad named Judith flew the coop."

Hagla reacts with such calm it is scary. Zenuvius even steps away.

"Judith escaped?" Hagla chokes on the words.

Wiggins is clueless.

"The fairies did it," Zenuvius grumbles.

SPTZZZT! A flick of Hagla's finger turns Wiggins into a crinkly black bug. He scurries into a crack in the wall before she can step on him.

The veins in Hagla's neck pop out as she turns to Mr. Snivels.

"Fairies?" Hagla snarls.

"They are from Bladderwhack pond, milady. The OTHER side," he responds nervously.

Hagla rushes to her cauldron. "Show me." She commands.

Curious, Wiggins creeps back into the room as Hagla watches Tip's face appear in the surface of the cauldron. This time it is from a higher viewpoint, like an owl is circling above their trailer. Before Wiggins can run away, Hagla zaps him back to normal.

"OUT! Back to work," she shouts.

"We didn't notice 'em before. Nobody goes into Bladderwhack on purpose," Mr. Snivels says meekly.

Hagla does a double take as Chloe moves into view.

"Who is the girl in the glasses?" Hagla is seriously worried. "I banished everyone with glasses. She can ruin everything! She could hear Judith's wailing."

Hagla stares at Chloe's image for several seconds before the color drains out of her wrinkled gray face. The silence is deafening.

"She must be new." Mr. Snivels mumbles.

"Impossible," Hagla snuffs. "My spells prevent

anyone from getting in or out of the province. Wait a minute. Tashuhunka has been hiding her."

Hagla stared at her again.

"Has she come of age?" She asks ominously.

"I am afraid we do not know much about her." Mr. Snivels says carefully.

Hagla's eyes narrow viciously and she strokes her scrawny cat who is eying a small rat.

"Well, no matter. We know how to get rid of pests, don't we Snickets?"

CHAPTER 10

I don't know where I am, the fog is so dense I can't see my feet. I feel a breeze brush by me. It scares me. I step lightly as I run. I'm not sure where the ground is or if there is ground. I have the eerie feeling that I am heading for a fall. I don't know why I forgot that I can fly.

Wicked frenzied shadows surround me, darkening the fog like storm clouds. In a FLASH they close in screeching and fluttering like attacking bats. I panic and run faster, but they catch up to me. I am terrified. I can't out run them. I don't know what to do. I give up. My knees collapse. I close my eyes, crouch down and shield my head with my arms.

OUT OF THE DARKNESS, a gentle hand touches mine and the fog disappears.

I feel strong arms wrap gently around my waist, pulling me close and caressing me as we float upward. I relax and open my eyes. Tash, I think. But it isn't. It's that guy.

My heart flutters when I realize it's him. He looks deep into my eyes like he is seeing...ME. Like he understands me. His gaze is open, non-judgmental and accepting.

His body is so warm. I melt, not literally, but being in his arms feels so right that my body succumbs. I felt at peace and I am drawn to him like nothing I've ever experienced before. He looks at me like he knows what he wants...me.

Suddenly, a look of absolute fear overtakes over his face. A horrified feeling pierces sharply into my soul. I have never felt so terrified.

"She's found you," he whispers.

My body starts jerking. I am in bed. Tip is shaking me by the shoulders.

"Chloe, wake up. You've got to see this."

As Tip drags me out of bed, I am still groggy and in ecstasy. When my butt hits the floor the warm fuzzy feeling from my dream is pretty much over.

Tip pulls back the curtains on the window. Ten large owls are perched in the pine trees across the road. More are landing in other trees.

I get up and stare out the window in disbelief. "Why are there so many of them?"

"It's like that old Alfred Hitchcock movie where birds attack a whole town," Tip says excitedly. "Only they weren't the size of Audis."

"They look hungry. Where's Pops?"

"At work. We, you, overslept. By the way, why were you moaning?"

She gives me that "knowing" glance. I blush. She grins wider. Thankfully Darling enters before I have to tell Tip about my dream. The poor thing is breathing hard. Darling only lives a little bit away, but with the owl assassins out there, it is amazing she had the guts to run the distance.

"I called my mom," she said catching her breath. "She said to wait for the wranglers. But look, the queen gave me fairy dust."

She proudly offers her small satin bag of the sparkling golden powder to us.

"Wow, the dust is hard to come by," I say, distracted by the owls.

Tip shuts the curtains. "Unfortunately, it's not enough."

Darling is disappointed.

"Thanks Darling. That's great. Save it for later." I tell her.

Scratchy feet on the roof make us look up.

"We're not safe here. Tip, where does Pops keep his keys?"

We dart for the garage and climb into Pop's bus. Something inside is yelling at me to get the heck out of there. I hold the key down so long that the engine makes that screeching, scraping sound of an overworked starter. The engine roars.

"The doors are shut."

Darling starts to get out.

"No. No time." I grind the bus into gear and crash right through the red wooden garage doors, bolting toward the road as fast as the rickety contraption can go. The old white bus is plastered with fluorescent flower power stickers and its wheel wells are covered with dried mud.

"This thing drives like it's glued together." I was half-complaining, half-explaining for why I am driving badly. The fact that giant predatory owls are chasing us with evil intentions doesn't dawn on me as an excuse. Probably blocking it out.

"Pops hasn't used this bus since his hippie days in '69 when he took the elderfairies to Woodstock." Tip said.

"I didn't know Pops was a hippie."

An owl that attacks the front window, claws out. I swerve hard to avoid it.

"Whoa. Hang on," I yell.

Owls dive at us, pecking and clawing at the roof, but the old metal holds firm. The back tire isn't so lucky. It punctures on a turn. I almost lose it. We swerve again. Owls land on the roof and pound on it trying to break in. The bus hits a rock popping a second tire.

"I know a short cut," I mumble softly, and turn off the road.

"Where are you going?" Tip shouts frantically.

"Shh. Don't make her nervous." Darling adds with very big eyes.

"We'll be a harder target in the woods," I explain. "Whoops." I should have warned her before we blasted through the creek. She falls on her butt. Two tires blow out. I'm not speculating on what caused them to pop, but the timing makes me laugh. Tip looks at me like I've lost my mind again.

I keep driving. We are on the rims, weaving around

trees and bushes through the forest. I cut through to the old road when a huge gray spotted owl catches up to us. It gets its claw around the luggage rack and is pecking into the roof. Another owl lands above me and pecks on the front window so hard it cracks. I swerve trying to throw the owls off but we almost roll over. The front window shatters and the angry owl is in my face. We scream. The owl snaps its beak at me narrowly missing my nose.

Something darts by.

Oh no! Tash!

I am worried for him. I had forgotten. I put him in danger by trying to escape. What if he gets hurt?

Suddenly, the owl is yanked out of my face and swung upside-down by a rope. I slam on the brakes. The owl is pulled up into the treetops, where it disappears.

Another owl attacks from the side, but it is caught in a noose and yanked into a spring-loaded cage–not Tash's method.

"Wranglers!" Darling exclaims.

REALLY OLD pot-bellied fairies riding screeching black crows swarm the bus. Like cowboy hustlers, they herd the owls into golden cages like it is old hat. The wrangler boss, Oldman Cooley, a weathery-faced man who is so thin he looks like you could blow him over, enters the bus.

"Are you girls all right?" Oldman Cooley asks with a Texan drawl.

"Yes, Mr. Cooley, thank you," I say gratefully.

Tip is thrilled to see them. Up until then we'd only

heard what I thought were puffed up stories about them at the elderfairies' Sunday afternoon card games. We'd never seen them in action.

"What will happen to the owls?" Tip asks curiously.

Mr. Cooley gets all wide-eyed like he is about to tell us a deep dark secret.

"That's the mystery of these woods. Come back in an hour and they'll all be gone! True as you and me. Legend has it, the mighty spirit takes them." He wheezes with a spooky voice.

"Mighty spirit?" Darling cracks sarcastically.

"Ah, they probably chew their way out." Tip said, not believing him either.

The wrangler looks at us with deadly seriousness, like he is about to reveal a great forbidden truth.

"Every time an owl disappears from one of these, the cages are still intact. Locks and all. Like magic." He says it as if it was a mystery to him as well.

I scan the woods slyly for Tash. I feel he is near, and I know he won't let the wranglers see him. He always told me he was certain that if anyone except me knew that he existed, his life would be in danger.

I remember a day when I was about twelve. I found an owl in a cage in the woods, not far from here. I knelt next to Tash as he waved an Indian charm in front of it, humming. The owl swayed peacefully.

"What are you doing?" I asked.

"A trick my grandfather taught me," he said proudly.

"The owls are illusions. A long time ago, Hagla cast a spell, changing harmless mice into the thing they fear the most. Then she forced them to spy for her."

After a moment, the owl turned into a mouse of a similar color. Tash smiled at it. "This breaks their trance," he told me. Then he told the mouse, "Go on. You're free." The mouse scurried out through the bars in the cage. Tash watched it scamper away, thoughtfully. I was so proud of him.

"I am impressed."

He sat up a little taller, like my words had a nice effect on him. It was a great moment. Tash looked at me as if he genuinely cared about me, then a second later shut down and pulled himself away.

"I should go."

He said it, but I knew he wanted to stay.

The loud twang of Mr. Cooley's voice shouting in my ear snaps me back to the moment. I must have not heard him the first couple of times.

"CHLOE! You with us now?"

"Uh, yes."

"As I was sayin', we'll escort you to town. You best stay there until we get the rest of them."

CHAPTER 11

The flower-power hippie bus backfiring up Main Street to the front steps of Penstemon Academy, surrounded by hooting elderfairy wranglers riding black crows brings the students to the windows, then out to the street.

I park the bus, then exit following Tip and Darling. Mrs. B and others crowd around the bus anxious to hear Oldman Cooley tell them the wranglers latest harrowing adventure. I'm still amped and I scan the trees for prying eyes as I make my way through the crowd. I see several white luxury cars parked in front of the school, but that unusual sight doesn't process, even as a passenger window rolls down when I approach.

"Girls, back inside please," Professor Boone commands in a lovely voice. "Time for class."

I am glad to be inside a big building with five levels and thick brick walls. I take my seat in class and look out the window where I had dreamed about that boy before.

Get a grip, Chloe. I focus back on the classroom and *Wha'?* Everyone is staring at me. I had forgotten all about my black eye.

Monica is absolutely delighted. "Lovely," she snarls.

Boone, professor of fashion and etiquette, walks over to my desk. She knows me pretty well.

"Flying too fast again?" She smirks.

Behind me, Priscilla, number two in Monica's clique, is swooning over a photograph of Prince Peter of Europe on the cover of the town tabloid, *HAG'S RAG*. Peter is wearing a full-length blue cloak and running away from the camera. You can't even see his face, just some blond hair where the wind is blowing his hood back. Priscilla is practically drooling. It's like she is about to lick the picture. She jumps out of her chair when Professor Boone taps her on the shoulder.

"Put that away, Priscilla."

Priscilla slides the magazine inside her desk.

"I realize we've had an eventful morning, but we have a full schedule. Quiet down, now." Professor Boone begins.

We hush.

Professor Boone looks at me and frowns. She taps me on the head with her wand and my black eye is healed. A second tap makes my hair curl.

Great, I think sarcastically.

"To make time for a treat," Professor Boone says smiling at me, "We will combine fashion and etiquette with horticulture 101. Professor Higglewitz?"

Professor Higglewitz, a short, round elderfairy, floats in followed by her teacher's aide—a bird named Riggs. She clasps her chubby little hands together with delight.

"It's bulb season. Who can tell me what that means?"

She shrills.

Priscilla stands up. "Put away your white shoes."

"Yes," Professor Boone nods as Priscilla sits down. "And skirt lengths are changing. Who knows what trends the designers are telling us about this season?"

Monica stands up, taking her know-it-all power stance.

"It's a trap. Never follow trends, unless it's a one night thing, like for a party. Remember the four "C's–Classic cuts, constant chic."

Good to know. I roll my eyes sarcastically.

Monica sits.

Tip stands and smiles at Professor Higglewitz.

"The arctic shift in the air currents stepping up a cold trend will entice earlier winter planting weeks before the storm season."

Not to be outdone, Monica stands when Tip sits down.

"Microfiber makes the best raincoats. It is lightweight and when treated, waterproof AND it won't wrinkle your clothing even in the heaviest downpours."

Tip and Monica bob up and down competing with each other like bobble-head car ornaments.

"Night rains and unseasonably cold temperatures can create leaf rot, fungus and plant diseases." Tip quips.

"Scented tissues are the best offense for anyone who is sensitive to decaying odors. We should all keep a pocket pack handy in case we run into anyone, I mean...thing, disgusting," Monica hisses.

Tip glares at her fearlessly.

"The well-saturated environment is abnormally ripe for increased bacterial larvae hatching. Foul parasites that pick dead skin cells off degenerating flesh and that are attracted to superficial smells."

"Okay," Professor Higglewitz sings nervously, "Everyone turn your textbooks to page thirty-seven. A recipe to protect against leaf rot and spidermites."

"Afterwards, we have a surprise. Prince Peter is coming to our class to tell us the latest from Europe." Professor Boone promises exitedly.

The Periwinkle fairies squeal with delight. I mean they actually squeal. I can't help it. I glance at Tip, wide-eyed, like *they've got to be kidding.*

Monica catches it. She sticks her nose up in the air and raises her hand. "Professor, can I do the spell?"

Professor Higglewitz is seriously surprised.

I should have suspected something was up.

"Why certainly Monica. It is wonderful of you to take an interest in something other than fashion."

Monica stands facing the class and raises her arms.

"From the seething biles of the underrealms I will you disgusting creature to be washed away!"

"Wha? Interesting words dear." Professor Higglewitz looks through the pages of her book.

Monica takes a pinch of fairy dust from her purse then blows it directly at me. Storm clouds form inside the room. Lightning cracks from the ceiling and burns a hole in my textbook. The other girls scream. Then, it rains ONLY on me.

"I'm not a spider mite."

"Whoops." Monica sneers slyly.

Professors Higglewitz and Boone are astonished.

"Where did you get fairydust?"

"My mother has connections," Monica snoots.

"You are worried where she got her fairydust – HELLO–It is raining on my head!" I don't really mind at this point. At least it is straightening my hair.

"Oh dear." Professor Higglewitz flutters frantically looking for something, then she waves a cloth over me, moving the air. The clouds evaporate and the rain stops.

"Monica, dear, you are not advanced enough to make up your own spells." Her voice is higher than usual.

"It's all right Monica. You certainly didn't mean to drench poor Chloe." Professor Boone has a soft spot for Monica. She rummages through the closet and finds some dry clothes for me to change into. "Here you are sweetheart."

"Why don't you zap her?" Darling asks.

"You know fairies are not supposed to use magic on each other–except for emergencies."

"Wow. I must have looked pretty bad before," I say, hoping for a compliment.

"Yes, dear. Well, take your time, fix yourself up," Boone says gently, scooting me toward the door.

Monica plays innocent.

"My bad. Sorry Pillywiggin." She flashes a sarcastic grin then changes to sweetness when the professors look.

Dripping like a drowned dormouse, sloshing shoes

and all, I am way past embarrassment as I head for the door.

It opens swiftly in front and I run smack into Prince Peter. I don't know who is more horrified. My hair made a big wet spot on his shirt.

"Oh, I'm sorry," I fumble, trying to dry him off but I am soaked so I'm not helping.

"It's fine," he smiles. "What is your name?"

"Chloe," I reply meekly out of embarrassment.

"Chloe," he repeats, grinning. "Do you cause chaos or does it find you?"

My heart sinks.

"You are very interesting," he whispers. Then he steps aside so I can leave.

Monica is so mad it looks like her head is going to blow off.

I head for the ladies room realizing that all my life I've felt that in the hierarchy of the universe–with the heroes, the scholars, the guides, and even the normal people making their way through life, bettering themselves on their spiritual path–I am the comic relief.

My squeaking shoes get really loud in the hallway. I catch a glimpse of myself in the reflection of the glass trophy cabinet. *Oh Boy.* This is definitely not one of my better days.

Just then, a dark shadow sweeps over my reflection. It gives me a chill, but is gone in an instant.

Great. I'm imagining things again.

As I near the end of the hall, the light dims and a sudden burst of wind slams a classroom door shut behind me. The lights flicker off and on and the sound of a thousand bats swirl around me.

Uh, yeah. I run.

I duck into the library and hide between the shelves. It is quiet in here. Whatever it was, it didn't follow me inside.

WHEW! I sink to my knees and take a long breath. A heavy thud from behind scares me. I drop the dry clothing, clench my fists and swing around fast—ready for whatever is to come.

It's just a book, lying on the ground.

Must have fallen off the shelf.

I pick it up and instantly know that was a really bad idea.

The book glows and then jolts out of my hands. It hovers in the air in front of me, then after a deceptive pause it sucks me inside.

The next thing I know I am falling from the sky—like in *"Alice in Wonderland"* or *"Chicken Little."* I don't know why I forgot that I can fly.

By the time I remember, it's too late. I crash onto a cart full of wooden chicken cages. Chickens scatter everywhere, squawking and clucking in a frenzy of feathers and hay.

"You can't just drop from the sky and smash my chickens!" A high-pitched voice with a Scottish accent screams. Elsie, a sweet-looking, but angry elderfairy herds her chickens with a large brimmed hat. "Who is going to pay for these cages?" She exclaims.

She grabs three hens but realizing she has no cages to put them in, lets them go. I catch a squawking chicken by the

99

leg as it pecks birdseed from my lap and offer it to her.

"Get up. Get up," she says impatiently. "You're not even supposed to be here. Who are you?"

"I'm sorry."

Birdseed, feathers and other things are stuck to my clothes. They don't fall when I stand up.

"My name is Chloe."

Elsie brushes me off.

"Well, Chloe, obviously your parents did not teach you the rules of proper etiquette. A refined lady does not crash onto people's belongings like a falling cow. You are a fairy aren't you? You can fly."

She gasps and gawks at the crest on my neck. She peers at it closely, and then looks me right in the eyes, nose to nose, with an astonished expression.

"You bear the mark," she whispers in amazement.

She whisks me across a narrow cobblestone street shielding me with her hat. I put my glasses back on as my feet try to catch up to the arm Elsie is pulling on.

Everyone in the street looks ancient, like they are in a time warp from the European Renaissance age. Except, the quaint windows of the shops all have flat-screen televisions in them and each one is tuned to a different TV network.

Newscasters are reporting events going on in the human world right now.

The first one reports, "Hurricane Carla breezes through southern Texas with little damage."

The second TV shows a United Nations dinner party

with dignitaries from all over the world. "We may finally have peace in the Middle East and Africa. After the Pre-Fab dinner party of the century thrown by the Coalition for Peace on Earth, a sudden and unusual change of attitude came over the dignitaries as they cracked open and read their fortune cookies. We should have ordered take-out at one of these things a long time ago," the newscaster reports.

The third screen stops me in my tracks. A guy with long blond hair swings a huge rock onto another, cracking it open. Smaller boys chip gems from it. An Oddizen guard snaps a whip above the boys heads. It is right out of my dreams.

"Those boys...Is that a new series?"

"You can see them?" Elsie is surprised. "That is not television dear, it is a direct feed."

"They're real?"

She glances up and down the street and into windows as if she is afraid of something.

"Oh yes. The boys are very real."

Are you kidding?

She opens the door of an old tavern and nudges me inside. "Quickly."

Eldon, the tavern innkeeper is extremely tall and rail thin with a long, pointed nose and twinkling eyes–definitely an ancient. One glance at Elsie dragging me into the back room and he walks away from a customer, mid-sentence.

More curious elderfairies cram into the tiny room, pushing and complaining as Eldon tries to shut the door.

Elsie pulls back my hair and shows them my birthmark. The crowd hushes instantly. I swat her hand away and pull my hair back over my neck.

"I know it's ugly, but there's no need to be rude."

"No, sweetheart, it is not ugly, the opposite actually," Elsie says with a nice tone to her voice. "We are admiring your birthmark. We have waited so long we had almost given up hope."

"Your destiny is written in the ancient prophecies, we just didn't expect for you to come here." Eldon sits down so we'd be eye level. "Feeling out of place I take it?"

That would be a yes.

"Everywhere you go, you are the strangeling, the odd one, welcome, but you have not found a place where you feel that you belong." He pauses, staring at me.

"She's come to save us," someone shouts from the back of the crowd.

George, a man with especially large ears and feet turns to Eunice, a frail-looking woman next to him, and cracks, "Come on the bus. What bus?"

I move closer to Elsie, trying not to get stepped on by George's over-sized wing-tipped shoes.

"Chloe," Elsie explains, "No one from outside this book can see or hear of the lost Shadow Boys."

"Lost Shadow Boys?"

"Yes, dear, the boys you saw. They nicknamed themselves Shadow Boys, probably to keep their spirits up in that horrid prison."

"What?" George shouts with frustration. "Can you all speak up? I can't hear a dang thing."

Eunice looks at him and shakes her head. "You've got your earpiece in backwards," she tisks.

"What?" He grumbles.

"Your earpiece." Eunice shouts. She takes it out, turns it around and puts it back in his ear. "It was backwards."

George nearly jumps out of his shoes.

"You don't have to yell for carps sake." He says crankily. He seems to see Chloe for the first time. "Why are you wet?"

"Come to my salon dear. We'll have you fixed up in a jiffy." Eunice tells me sweetly.

"There isn't time for that Eunice," Eldon warns.

"Thirty-seven minutes. Has she been here longer than thirty-seven minutes? Get her out of here or she'll be stuck with us." George is suddenly frantic.

Eldon and Elsie are the only calm ones in the room.

"Chloe," she says secretively. "Do you realize that you are the only one free who can see or hear things clearly? Hagla's spells infected the entire realm. She wiped out all memories of the boys and what came before."

"Her spells prevent people from hearing or seeing the truth of it." Eldon says as he examines my glasses. "Her magic can't get through the reflection."

"That's why we were put in this dang book," George whines, putting on his reading glasses. "You know the eyesight is the first to go...but I could tell you some stories," he winks.

Eldon shifts uncomfortably at George's twinkling grin then nods at the elderfairies to leave. As the last person exits, he turns to me seriously.

All I can think of is, *Uh-oh*.

"Chloe, sometimes we have to delay what is important to us to do what is right."

Suddenly, I have a bad feeling in my stomach.

"Your path is not certain. You may continue to search for your parents. You may attempt to save the lost Shadow Boys. You may fail at both."

The last to leave, George pokes his head back in.

"Give her a little encouragement why don't ya?" He cracks. Elsie gently pushes him out and shuts the door.

"I can't save anybody. I wouldn't even know where to begin." *Save the lost Shadow Boys, WHAT?*

A look of shock comes over Eldon's face. "You freed Judith?" He is delighted.

"It was an accident," I admit.

"She fulfilled the first prophecy!" Elsie gasps. "Do you think...?"

Eldon's glare at her stops her from finishing.

"How do you know about Judith?"

"I hear thoughts and see visions, Chloe. A gift we have in common. You are just learning of yours. Do not have fear."

He removes a pendulum from his pocket and holds its chain between his fingertips. It circles clockwise very fast but when he moves it toward me it stops sharply. Elsie and Eldon exchange puzzled glances.

"When I was your age, and coming in to my gifts, I was apprehensive too. This pendulum helped me sort it all out." He moves it close to his chest and it spins clockwise. "It's just a trick. I don't use it much anymore, except to find my keys," he grins.

I can tell they are keeping something from me. Eldon moves the pendulum next to my shoulder. The point on its crystal points down strongly like it is attached to the ground by an invisible string. It does the same thing above my head. He moves it toward himself and it circles, then it stops when he moves it back toward me.

"What's wrong?" I can tell he is concerned.

"The pendulum spins on energy. It moves clockwise for positive, counterclockwise for negative."

He focuses on it like he was trying to make it spin next to me. "It seems, Chloe, that you do not have a charge."

Huh? What do you say to that?

"That is impossible Chloe, Eldon is mistaken. Every thing has an electromagnetic charge." Elsie says briskly.

She takes the pendulum from him and tries it herself. It does the same thing. Next to her it spins. Next to me it hangs still as if it is stuck.

Eldon squints at me.

"I cannot get past her present thoughts. Chloe, someone has gone to great lengths to hide you."

I cleared my mind. A trick Tash, taught me, to hide

him.

"There is a very old feel to this." Eldon seems surprised as he says it. He looks at Elsie and then at me, curiously, like I'm something scary. He catches himself and covers the fear with a smile so as to not hurt my feelings.

"Where are you from Chloe?"

"Penstemon."

He shakes his head, no. "Are you certain? Who are your parents?"

"You cannot see that?" Elsie asks astonishingly.

Eunice peeks back into the room.

"Her spies are back," she whispers fearfully. "Who else knows you are here?" Eldon asks.

"No one. I found the book by accident."

"Believe me, that was no accident."

CHAPTER 12

Meanwhile, back at Penstemon Academy, the bell rings ending the morning break. Darling and Tip remove Hall Monitor vests and give them to a teacher. In the cafeteria, girls are clamoring around Prince Peter. He reacts sweetly although he seems eager to get away. He glances at his attendant like it's a signal for help.

Professor Boone notes his need for a rescue and says, "Girls, break is over. Please return to your classrooms."

"Where is she?" Darling huffs impatiently.

"I'll find her," Tip replies equally concerned, or ticked, then speeds into the hall. Darling is about to re-enter the classroom, when Monica blocks her path.

Peter, about to enter the hall, slyly steps back and motions for his attendant to stop. He seems a bit delighted at the argument and listens peering carefully around the corner.

"I take it the hall monitor duty was your idea?" She grumbles. Darling may be small, but she is brave.

"No one embarrasses me and gets away with it. There will be consequences, severe consequences." Monica hisses.

Darling exhales slowly. "Just walk away," she says under her breath.

Monica needles her. "Darling, I hate to be the one to tell you, but if your wings haven't matured by now, they're not going to. You'll never be able to fly."

"I'm not going to listen to you Monica. You're evil."

Monica poses with her pinky to the corner of her mouth, like that character in that Mike Myers movie.

Darling stands strong, crossing her arms over her belly.

"Pudgy little thing. It would take a crane to lift your lard butt off the ground," Monica sneers.

Darling takes a step toward the class.

"Where did motor-mouth, uh, Tart... Tip run off to? What is she, like a walking dictionary? Does she ever shut up? And Chloe Pillywiggin. HA! She is a walking joke. Way too easy to humiliate. You misfits stay away from me, or your lives will be a nightmare."

"That's it." Darling never gets mad, but Monica has gone too far, this time. She says, "You are mean, rude, and have a bad 'tude. The world would be better without you in it." Darling blows the Queen's fairy dust on her. "Monica, you're FIRED!"

Peter stops his laugh not wanting to be caught.

Monica watches herself be erased from the feet up, disappearing before Darling and Peter's horrified eyes.

"Uh-oh," Darling gulps.

Back inside the book, a fast-paced thumping grows louder and louder until the tavern door slams open and George runs in from the street.

"Someone is holding the book!" he says excitedly. "Where is the girl?"

Eunice enters the tavern from a side door, delighted with herself. An old woman dressed in my clothes follows her. "Edna will be our decoy. See? I told you I could be quick."

She has to pull me into the room. She had cleaned me up, styled my hair, adding hair clips and streams of colors, then dressed me in new shoes and an outfit that was tighter and shorter than I had ever worn before. For the first time in my life I feel...pretty. It's weird, in a nice way. George is especially delighted.

"If only I was 200 years younger, we could have a time! I'm a dancer, you know."

I think he meant it as a compliment.

Then, wasting no time, Edna, George and two male elderfairies, hustle out the front door, and fly quickly down the street.

Seconds later, two dark faeries screech past the tavern window chasing them.

"Dark faeries?" I didn't mean to say that outloud.

Elsie doesn't even shush me, she just glares at me to keep quiet.

Spooky creatures, I had heard about them, but had never seen one before. Their skin is dark gray, almost purple and their eyes are black and hollow as if they have no souls—or if they do, they are the darkest evil you can imagine.

Eldon and Elsie shield me from view as they pass.

After a moment, Eldon sneaks into the street to make sure it is clear, then waves to us. Tash's face fills up the sky. As soon as I see him I am pulled upward.

Eldon tugs on my foot. "Not yet."

Tash's fingers are grabbing my hand.

Eldon pulls me back down.

"Chloe, Judith will not survive without her essence," he says urgently. "You are the only one who can help her. Hagla's spells will have affected her by now. Even she will have forgotten all about the boys."

Tash pulls me up, Eldon pulls me down. I feel like a yo-yo.

"Where is it? Her essence," I ask.

"I do not know."

"Do you have a hunch?"

"Tell her the rest of the prophecy, she has a right to know," Elsie says ominously. The futility in her voice sinks in like a warning.

Tash pulls harder.

Eldon loses his grasp.

In an instant, I am pulled up and out of the book, but the expressions on their faces are giving me chills.

I trip or fall and knock Tash down, landing on top of him. The book snaps itself shut and slides onto the top level of the bookshelf.

I realize that I am on top of him. Tash looks surprised.

"Wow," he says softly.

I don't think he meant to say it out loud. He blushes and stares at me. I think he smells me. Okay, now I'm nervous. I roll off him and sit up.

"You couldn't have waited for him to answer?"

"Who?" Tash is still holding my hand. He realizes it but doesn't let go.

I stand up, just as Tip enters the library. She sees the top of my head.

"Chloe, is that you? What have you been doing?"

"Get rid of her," Tash whispers before he ducks behind the bookcase to hide.

"You were only supposed to..."

I step out to confront her.

Tip stops cold at the sight of me. "Whoa. What happened to you?"

"You don't want to know."

I leave with Tip quickly so she wouldn't spot Tash and run into Peter as he walks toward the main doors with his entourage. He stops cold when he sees me. His expression changes from surprise to a wide grin. "Chloe, you are definitely interesting." His attendant ushers him out.

Darling enters the hall and runs up to me with a terrified look on her face.

"I didn't mean to do it," she whimpers.

"Do what?" I ask.

"Monica. I erased her."

I look in the classroom and Monica is sitting at her desk, cooing at the broadcast from the fashion show.

"What do you mean? She's right there."

"You see her? Where?"

"There. In her seat."

Unfortunately, Monica overhears us. "Oh my gaad. You can see me?" She leaps up from her desk and scoots into the hall, practically pouncing on me. "Tell the toddler to change me back." She gives my outfit the once over. "And give me the number of your dresser."

"You see Monica?" Darling asks.

"Unfortunately."

"Darling, we're not supposed to use magic except for emergencies." Tip warns.

"It was an accident. I told ya."

I am running out of time to find Judith's essence.

"I have to go." I hurry to the main doors.

"Tell the Professors I had an emergency."

"What do we do about Monica?" Darling asks.

"Hide her. Until you figure it out."

"Hide her? Monica's invisible."

"Chloe's really starting to worry me," Tip sighs. That piques Monica's curiosity.

"Why? What's going on?" Seeing that she won't get any answers from them, she follows me.

CHAPTER 13

Jayce leans against the bars of his cage in a depressed lump when flickering light catches his gaze. A shadow blocks the light on him. LB pushes his face out from it.

"What are you doing? They'll catch you. We need to keep our abilities a surprise." Jayce whispers harshly.

"For what? Our funeral? We've got to send someone to convince Chloe to come." LB argues.

"Tash hasn't told her about us." Jayce finally levels with him. He is seething.

"What?"

"He suddenly decided she might not be the one."

"Oh yeah. There must be a gazillion girls up there with the crest of Fairydom on their necks. Sure, he just picked wrong."

Jayce looks at him seriously, apologizing in his way. "She's not coming," he says softly.

"The guys won't fight without her."

"LB. Use the tunnel. Get out while you can."

"What? No." LB says anxiously.

"Tell Parker it's time for the draw."

LB understands what that means. His chin begins to quiver and tears well up in his eyes. He fights to control it.

"The dragons haven't come back yet. Tash may have caught them," Jayce continued. "There may still be time to get men out the tunnel."

"No. I won't leave you."

"It's over, LB," Jayce means it. "After tomorrow we're food."

"So we'll fight. We all go together, that's the plan. That's always been the plan."

Jayce can't look at him. This is breaking his heart.

"LB, please. Don't make it harder than it is," he says. "Some of us have to survive this."

"We will," LB says bravely. "Forget the prophecies. We'll make our own destiny." He says it with such determination, it makes Jayce smile.

"I told you that when you were a kid."

"I remember. It's like our slogan," LB whispers with effect, "We are Shadow Boys. We make our own destiny."

"That's right. And your destiny is to get out of here, alive. Make the draw."

LB sadly turns to leave.

"Hey." Jayce grabs him through the bars and holds him tightly. "I'm really gonna miss you."

Inside the Shadow Boys cave, LB stands in the middle of the elite team–Parker, Leo, Beav and Max. The mood is solemn to say the least.

"No way." Leo says firmly. "I'm not doing it."

Beav folds his arms, "Me neither."

"It's an order," Parker commands softly. "We've got to put it to the men."

"I did," Max replies reading text messages. "Nobody's going."

"We stay together, that's the plan." LB agreed.

Parker thinks for a moment. "This is insane. We fight we lose. We stay we lose. At least with the draw, some of us will get out."

"We could win." The guys look at Leo like he is crazy. "We have to stay positive," he says.

Beav shakes his head. "Your zen crap's crap. We're done. It's over. We're dead."

"Great attitude, Beav."

"He's right. We'll never win unless we take Jayce out of the picture." Parker huffs.

"What?" LB can't believe he said that.

"Every time the guards grab one of us Jayce gives up. He protects us at all costs. To beat them, something's got to change." Parker complains.

"You're sure Chloe's not coming?" Max asks.

"That was a fairytale," Beav growls.

"Max, come on." Leo shakes his head. "It was just a lame story. A GIRL, comes down HERE and saves us. You can't tell me you really believed that?"

"We all did. You too." Max argues.

"Yeah, well a lot of good it did us." Leo throws a pack at Beav. "Let's get the gear ready."

They walk into another cavern.

"We could try to find Chloe," LB offers.

"Why? You know magic doesn't work down here. What's she going to do that we haven't tried already?" Parker huffs.

"Okay. So you think that. To the rest of the guys she is a symbol for hope. Hope has kept us alive this far." LB is really reaching. He doesn't want to give up yet.

Parker chuckles at him.

"Come on, Parker," LB pleads. "You said in order to beat them something had to change."

"Even if we could get to her, if someone goes missing the witch will kill all of us. We might as well do the draw." Parker reminds him.

"So, send someone that won't be missed," LB says cheerfully.

Hal is asleep on the floor, next to the showers. Mist from the steaming slate blows on him. "No, thank you. I'm already wearing Chanel No. 5," Hal coos.

LB creeps up to him silently.

Sensing LB right in his face, Hal opens one eye, then the other. The take charge expression on LB's face makes Hal suspicious.

"I am not going to like this am I?"

CHAPTER 14

Meanwhile, topside, in front of Penstemon Academy, Tash sneaks up behind me. "Shhh. Quick, follow me."

I pause, wondering if I should tell him what is happening or keep him out of it.

"Come on. It's not safe here," Tash insists.

He inserts an ancient-looking key into a notch in a tree and opens its trunk like a door.

Inside, narrow hand-carved stairs, lead downward.

"Tuck in your wings," he whispers.

He pushes me in quickly and shuts the door behind us. It is pitch black. He takes my hand, leading me down. At the bottom, he lights a lantern.

"Gnomes made these tunnels."

"Gnomes don't exist."

"Maybe not now. But they once did."

He looks back, and up at the door.

"Did you hear that?"

"Hear what?"

Little did we know Monica is outside trying to pick the lock with a bobby pin.

A crinkly black bug crawls over my foot. I gasp and stomp at it. Tash stops me.

"No." He says urgently. "Nothing here is as it seems. Could be someone you know."

"Okay, that's creepy. Can we go?"

"Yeah."

Tash glances suspiciously behind us, and then takes off running down the dark, narrow tunnel. I run on my tiptoes, trying as much as possible not to touch the ground or squish anything...body.

We climb more stairs and crawl out of a stump near Tash's camp, which was now deeper in the woods. I am sooo happy to be out of there.

"Our camp, you moved it. Or, your camp. It's so nice."

Everything is made from nature, a sink, a shower, a padded hammock, cabinets in an old log, and the old teepee that we first lived in, camouflaged with wild blackberry strands, ferns and flowering vines.

"Tash, this is beautiful. Much better than the last one."

"Chloe, that was years ago." Tash pulls a vine that lifts a piece of ground up.

"Yes, I know."

A hole in the ground is lined with cedar and neatly

filled with books, boxes, tools, twine, ropes, arrows and small hatchets. He wastes no time, knowing which carefully latched box to open as he fills his satchel.

I reach for a box with a photo of an Indian woman.

"You framed your mother's picture. It's lovely."

"Please don't touch anything."

"I was worried about you this morning."

"Don't be." Tash drops his satchel. "Shhh."

He disappears before my eyes. I hear a WHHEEE and a ZIP, and then smoke billows from behind Tash's tent.

"Are you trying to burn the place down?" Tash sounds angry.

I peek through a bush and see a dragon with little wings dangling upside-down in a net from a charred tree branch. The dragon is much smaller than the one that chased me, but a dragon none-the-less. Tash is patting dirt on the branch trying to put the last of the hot embers out. He isn't afraid of the dragon at all. In fact, he is miffed at it. I realize that he has been keeping secrets from me. He obviously knows this dragon.

"What were you thinking?" Tash scolds him. "Hagla's spies might see you."

"The lads sent me. This Chloe person is supposed to be the real schlemiel."

He bobs up and down as Tash loosens the net.

"She hasn't come into her powers yet," Tash huffs. "Besides, it's going to take more than one fairy to get them out. How many times have I tried before?"

The dragon hits the ground with a thud, then stands up quickly.

"Dude, take a chill pill. We know you've tried but we're out of time. We need her."

"She's clueless." Tash says it so sharply.

I lose my footing and tumble through the bush, falling face first at their feet. The dragon is so startled he falls backward and accidentally flames Tash's right butt cheek.

"Hey!"

Tash jumps and grabs onto the burnt tree branch, which unfortunately breaks from his weight. Tash lands on his feet with only a medium-sized hole in his pants.

I look up at them and blow a leaf off my nose. He is so mad and I can't help but laugh.

"Oh, yeah. She's the real schlemiel." He reaches down to help me up.

"I can do it myself." I tell him sharply, remembering he had just insulted me twice. I stand up then, duck behind Tash when the dragon moves toward me.

"It's okay, he's harmless."

The dragon gives him a dirty look.

"I don't mean harmless, exactly." Tash backpedals.

"I have been known to make a mean burger," the dragon grins.

"Hal's a friend. Fairydragon, last of his kind."

"Tashuhunka, Indian warrior. Legend in his own mind."

"Hey."

"Hal. I like you already." I offer my handshake, awkwardly, suddenly unsure whether he is able to use his arms like that, but he shakes my hand like it is old hat.

"I'm Chloe. And I would be honored to help, any way I can."

Tash is unimpressed.

"You don't know what you're talking about."

Tash storms off toward his camp holding his hand over his exposed buttocks.

I ignore him and chat with Hal as we follow. "Will you take me to the Shadow Boys?"

Tash stops in his tracks and asks with astonishment, "How do you know about the Shadow Boys?"

"The elderfairies in the book."

"You didn't tell her?" Hal is surprised to say the least.

"He doesn't talk to me," I tell him.

"She wasn't ready. She's still not ready."

"Well, I've seen them," I reveal, finally. "Their leader, what's his name?"

"Jayce." Hal says proudly.

"Jayce." *What a nice name.* "He's come to me in dreams."

Tash's jaw drops. "What? You've been dreamwalking?" His voice cracks. "With JAYCE?"

"Whoa, Dad."

"I can help," I say.

"You can't go down there. Not without a plan." This time he is really mad. Tash grabs a pair of pants and steps behind a nearby bush to change. It is too short, but he wants to stay in the conversation so he crouches, mostly.

"What's the plan?" I ask. I can tell by the way Tash avoids eye contact with me that he doesn't have one. "You don't have a plan? No wonder you need me."

"We've had plans, lots of plans." Tash says testily. "That's the point. None of them worked."

"Obviously, you haven't thought of a good one. Okay, maybe that's harsh, but how could you keep secrets from me? What else haven't you told me?"

"Some things are better kept secrets," he says glaring guiltily at Hal. "Don't look at me that way. You don't know the whole story."

Hal doesn't say a word. He doesn't have to. His silence is making Tash extremely uncomfortable. I can tell that Hal thought I knew all about the boys. I wonder what else I am supposed to know.

"Chloe, stay here. I will get them out." Tash said.

"But the prophecies say I'm supposed to save them."

"How did you find out about the prophecies?"

I can see I am getting nowhere with Tash. I turn to the fairydragon. "Hal, do you know where Judith's essence is?"

"Judith?" Tash gasps.

"Yes, Supreme Fairy and Guardian of the Light."

"What is that? A new spa treatment?"

Oh no. That voice makes me cringe. Monica barges into the camp. Of course, I am the only one who can see her.

"Judith's alive?" Hal tears up.

Monica gives Tash a very slow once over–TWICE.

"ME-OW!" Monica gawks. "Is that who I think it is? He's real? Tash-U-HUNK-a."

"Why are you here?" I ask her. This is not good. And to make matters worse, Tash thinks I am talking to a tree.

"What are you doing?" He asks, walking to me while tying the zipper-like string on his pants.

"Monica's stalking me." I tell him, watching Monica drool.

"Tashuhunka and I have that in common. Hasn't he been watching you your whole life, like some kind of perv?"

She has a really devilish smile on her face.

"He's not a perv."

Tash glares at me for an explanation.

"Darling erased Monica so she's invisible to everyone but me."

"If you won't tell me the truth, don't talk to me."

"Seriously."

He looks around for Monica.

"She's right next to you."

Monica tries to touch him.

"Stop that."

"Now I understand why you've kept him for yourself. Yummy." She laughs.

Tash goes back to his "treasure trunk" in the ground.

"So what are we doing? Scavenger hunt?" Monica asks excitedly.

Tash watches me while he slots an arrow. "She's your

enemy. She could mess up the mission." He slides it into his satchel.

"So you are going to help find Judith's essence?" I ask him.

"If you tell me how you suddenly know all of this."

"Can you guys speak up? You're cutting in and out like a bad cellphone connection."

Tash packs his satchel and straps on weapons like he is readying for war.

"How can you hear the truth?" I asked him.

"The witch's spells don't affect me. Indian wisdoms."

I pick up one of his arrows and hand it to him, helping. "Wow, these would be so much better shooting down oranges than the pencils gave me to use."

He jerks it from my hand and throws it into a rock, showing me how sharp it is–like I am too young or inept to handle it. "No."

"Why are you so mad? I'm the one who should be mad. Why haven't you told me any of this before? You could have trained me."

"Trained you for what?" Monica sneers slyly.

"You think I'm that lame?"

Tash turns away.

Monica is delighted. If she made another rude comment, I didn't hear her, I am focused on Tash. I get in right in front of him.

"If you knew about the boys how could you just leave them there?"

"I didn't."

"Why you didn't tell me?"

"What do you think you can do?"

"Help."

"You have no idea what you're saying." He walks around me and ties the door shut on his teepee.

"What? Are you jealous? You can't save them so no one can?"

He looks at me like he is going to tell me something, but then shuts down. "It's complicated."

"You're scared."

"Okay, Chloe," he confesses coldly. "You're right. I am scared. You want to know the truth? Do you want to know what is written in the prophecies about your destiny?"

"Yea-ah." I say snottily.

Tash leans close and glares at me eye to eye. "You try to save them...and you DIE."

"So much for the sugar-coating." Hal quips.

I am stunned, but the fact that Hal is shocked too, tells me that Tash has kept this little tidbit from both of us.

"I've been trying to think of another way." Tash says to Hal remorsefully.

"I get it," Hal nods. "And the lads would have never let her come if they knew the truth. They would have given up."

"There's got to be another solution." Tash says firmly.

"Her path is predestined. You cannot ignore the fact that she found out about them in spite of you."

I have never seen Tash look desperate before.

Suddenly everything is clear to me. "That's why you stay away from me and why my parents haven't come for me...Why get attached, right?"

"I'm your protector. Not your boyfriend."

My hands start shaking. I sit down abruptly as my knees give out.

Tash drops his satchel and kneels in front of me, trying to calm me by steadying my hands. "The prophecies could be wrong." He says softly.

Monica practically falls over herself trying to get back into the conversation. "If he's not your boyfriend can I have him?"

I blank out for a moment. I have to face it. "I get it. I'm perfect for this. Who would miss me? Sure maybe friends for a little while, but up to this moment, my life hasn't mattered, really. Now it does." I stand up and step away from Tash.

"Chloe. No," he says.

My brain kicks into overdrive. Everything I've learned suddenly falls into place.

"Judith's wand and essence must be in Hagla's Castle. She must have a lab. I'll bet she keeps them there. That would be where I'd keep something that important...if I had a lab."

"You're kidding." Tash says, trying to convince me it is a stupid idea.

"It's my destiny to help those guys, like you said," I try hard to be optimistic. "Maybe I can skip dying part, or put it off until after. Hal, can you get me in?"

"No, but Tash can."

Tash argues against it. "I can't believe you're thinking of going to the Twisted Castle. Chloe, people don't come out of there."

"A twisted essence of light in a jar. Wicked. Count me in," Monica exclaims brainlessly.

"Monica, it's not a face cream, and you can't go."

"You're not getting rid of me."

"She can't come with us," Tash commands.

"That's what I just said."

"Have you two tried counseling?" Monica snoots.

Tash succumbs to my frustrated expression.

"Can you at least tell her not to talk to you?" he asks. "It's confusing."

"He's not a multi-tasker I take it." Monica laughs.

CHAPTER 15

A crescent moon hangs low over the Heatherworld. Tash has tied six magnets on bushes and is hanging upside-down from a tree branch positioning a seventh magnet to complete a circle. He finishes tying it in place then jumps down, landing silently, and admires his work.

I don't get it. "That's pretty."

Monica is gawking at him like he is a designer mark down sale at Neiman Marcus. Tash tosses a pebble just outside the circle of magnets. The pebble sparks when it hits and bounces back five feet. As we are gasping, Tash walks calmly through the circle of magnets, unharmed.

"The charge between the magnets knocks out the energy of the force field. Come on. It's safe," he smiles.

I look back at it as we climb up the rocky hill to the Heatherworld. "You're just going to leave it open like that? What if somebody finds it?"

"What if we have to get out in a hurry?" He replies.

Neither thought is comforting. I decide it's best to stop thinking altogether.

Tash crawls on his belly at the top of the ridge and looks through binoculars at the barren valley surrounding Hagla's Twisted Castle. When he waves, we sneak up next to him. Monica is shocked at the sight of it.

"It's all rocks. Where's the heather?"

It is probably a good thing he can't hear her.

"Fly low. Stay in the shadows," Tash whispers.

Mercenary dragons of every variety and emaciated black crows almost the size of Hal, fly in circular patterns, glaring at the ground. A crow dives and comes up a moment later with a mouse, nearly torn in half, in his beak.

Monica panics.

"All this for a spa treatment? I heard Hagla is evil with a capital EEK. What is this wanding thing and when did you start caring about your hair?"

"I am so glad you came." She is so ridiculous she makes me laugh. That breaks the ice. We share a rare moment where we don't want to kill each other. Tash looks at me like I've lost my mind.

"Ooh, we need outfits!" Monica squeals excitedly.

"You have more fairy dust?" I ask her.

Tash perks up. "How much?"

"Cost a fortune." Monica says proudly.

"Can you make me invisible?" I ask.

"Only if I can make it permanent. Seriously, I wish I knew how."

Okay, our fluffy moment is over.

"Not enough," I tell Tash.

"Stay close," he says. He flies quickly, leading us to the valley floor. I let Hal pass, then, tug on Monica to stop.

"I have an idea. Come on." I whisper to her.

"I prefer to stay with hunkadunka."

"No, come on."

"But we are supposed to stay together. It's safer that way." She is really scared.

"Monica, you're invisible, remember? The crows can't see you."

"Oh...yeah."

When Tash turns around, we are gone. He is shocked. "She ditched me."

"Can you blame her? You stick to her like hot gum." Hal snickers.

"She's gonna mess it up," Tash replies angrily, scanning the rocks for me. He and Hal duck between large boulders at the base where the Twisted Castle spirals up from the ground.

"What's with you?" Hal asks. "I've never seen you so cranky." Then it dawns on him. "Oh-Ho! You have the hots for her!"

"What? No no no. No way." Tash rolls his eyes at the goofy expression on Hal's face. "I just don't want her to get killed on my watch."

"Uh-huh."

"No, Hal."

"Uh-huh. Now I understand why you push her away." Hal sneers. Tash waits for the insight. "You're a wusse." Hal teases. "Get over yourself. If you want her, drop the attitude."

"I can't want her."

He says it so seriously and with such pent-up emotion Hal stops teasing him.

"Yeah. Well, then let her show you what she's learned, whether she knew you were teaching her or not."

Tash looks above them, wide-eyed. "I didn't teach her that."

Monica, now visible in a full body latex spa technician costume, carries a pink suitcase as she floats upward toward the castle entrance. Crows and dragons hover behind her and the castle guards watch with amazement that someone is actually visiting the Twisted Castle on their own accord.

Monica lands on the porch apprehensively. A firefly buzzes a light next to the front door. In a snap, it is sucked inside a crack in the wall by a long, blue tongue. Monica shudders.

"You so owe me, Pillywiggin," She says under her breath.

Before she can knock, Mr. Snivels opens the door. She perks up and hands him a business card.

"I have a gift for the lady of the manor." She tries not to gasp when she sees the old wicked hag herself hobbling toward the door with cash in her hand.

"Two boxes of thin mints, dearie," Hagla cackles.

Monica shakes her head, "No."

"No cookies?" Hagla whips out her wand and points it threateningly. Monica quickly shoves a business card in her face.

"Something better." Monica chirps. "An in-home spa treatment…Complimentary, of course. A gift."

Hagla smiles at Mr. Snivels. He has nothing to do with it, but takes the credit and grins nervously. Monica breezes in, playing her part perfectly.

"This will be fun." Monica presses a button on her case and giggles as her spa kit unfolds like a gun-belt of beauty aids. She sets it on top of the pink suitcase.

"Mr. Snivels please fetch the spa lady some tea." Hagla bats her eyes like a little girl as she sits in a recliner.

Mr. Snivels watches Monica with a glare in his eyes, then leaves. Monica kicks the suitcase as she places cucumber slices on Hagla's eyes and a headset connected to an I-pod over her ears.

"Wunnerful." The witch is relaxed already.

Monica snaps latex gloves on, then reluctantly touches Hagla's brittle hair, distracting her while I crawl out of the suitcase and sneak toward the stairs.

"I take it you've never heard of conditioner," Monica snoots under her breath.

"Hmm?" Hagla hums happily.

I am almost to the stairs when Hagla sits up.

"Where is that man? What, is he making it from scratch?"

Monica quickly slaps more conditioner on her hair and turns her head back around. "You will not believe the difference this creme will make on your hair."

"It feels marvelous." Hagla coos. She sits back and zaps a tea and dessert setting on top of the end table. "Eclair?"

CHAPTER 16

I duck into the stairwell and fly quickly up the stairs, trying not to make a sound—or look at the hideous orange paisley velvet wallpaper. I know that to an intruder, her laboratory will be the most dangerous room in the Twisted Castle and the route to it, will most certainly be rigged or bugged. I wonder what I am flying into and try to think of all the things that might be in the lab that I will need to avoid. I had heard rumors about dangers inside the Twisted Castle, but I don't notice the walls moving until I get dizzy.

Come on, Chloe, it's an optical illusion, I tell myself.

I fly to the ceiling and feel my way along the corner, to the top. It looks like my hands are bleeding, but they aren't. It is another illusion. I shut my eyes. The farther I fly upward, the more my stomach knots. Then, the echo of clanging keys startle me.

I open my eyes just in time to see four dragon guards crossing in a hallway on the level directly ahead of me. They enter a room. I crawl along the wall just above the door, trying not to make any noise, or wind. When I am far enough on the other side, I make a beeline for the top floor.

A high-pitched, whining sound pounds my head, and my skin feels like something is pricking it, but I keep going.

The stairs lead to a mezzanine. It is strangely quiet. The large stark room has wide stairwells at each of the five corners. One stairwell, labeled the South Tower in Celtic letters, is smaller, darker and looks a thousand years older than the others. I run into the creepy one.

This is it, I feel sure of it.

The stone stairs spiral straight up, leading to one door at the top. Mr. Snivels comes out of it suddenly. There is no place to hide. I dart to the ceiling and watch him waddle beneath me, hoping he doesn't look up. As soon as he has his back turned, I dash into the room. He shuts the door, unintentionally locking me inside!

Turning around, I see it is her lab, but it's decorated with incredibly comfortable furnishings. The room is dimly lit by candles and moonlight that is shining in through tall open windows. Bottles, jars and books are strewn on tables and bookshelves. A leopard print sofa with tabloids tracking Prince Peter's moves through Europe spread over it grace a fireplace where a large photo of Hagla, retouched to the point of fantasy, seems to glare at me where ever I move–just like in the movies. Jewels are arranged in a bowl on a table, next to the cauldron.

When I touch the cauldron, it glows.

I wonder. "Cauldron. Show me the wand of the Supreme Fairy and Guardian of the Light."

The liquid in the cauldron turns black.

"Where is Judith's essence?"

Nothing. I've never commanded a cauldron. They don't teach that in fairy school. I decide to do it like in the movies.

"Where is Judith's essence? Show me. I command you."

The cauldron flares up. Ultraviolet magic light swirls upward threateningly with a haunting laugh.

I back up and knock into a cabinet. It starts to fall. I steady it, but accidentally elbow a statue. Catching that, I turn it left then right trying to keep it from falling.

"Break it why don't ya?" Tash stands gallantly in the open window.

I won't admit it but I am glad to see him.

"Hey," he complains, "The first rule of a mission is to stick to it. No surprises."

"I think I liked you better when you were quiet."

Tash jumps down and walks to me, taking note of Hagla's potions and dried dead creature parts.

"Hey Chloe, I'm sorry. I should have told you..."

"Don't worry about it," I say, hiding my hurt feelings, "You were just doing your job."

I shift the statue back to the center. A second later a wall safe opens revealing an eerie demented-looking shrine. Photos are taped to the walls with Gaelic symbols and black magic charms tied to wicked looking boxes.

"Dark faery spells," Tash warned. "Don't touch them."

"No kidding." The whole thing gives me the chills. I look for Judith's essence. It has to be here.

A loud dragonshrill rips through the air. I recognize the roar. "That's the dragon that chased me."

"It's Zenuvius! Come on."

A small pouch that is tied with a leather string and some strands of brown hair catches Tash's attention. He snatches it quickly.

"I thought you said not to touch them."

"I said for YOU not to touch them," he smirks, but the careful way he holds the pouch in his palm and how he studies it, tells me it is of great importance.

"What is that?"

"A spell the witch cursed Jayce with so he has to obey her."

"How do you know it's the right one?"

The pouch is a little plainer than the others, but most have hair like this one.

"The leather string. He used to tie his pants with it."

"What is he tying his pants with now?"

"What?"

Okay maybe that is odd question. I guess my mind is wandering so I won't be so scared.

"Nevermind. Can you break the spell?"

"I don't know black magic."

I reach for the pouch.

"What happens if we untie it?"

"Don't!" Tash pulls it away quickly. "What if that kills him?"

Tash gently tucks the cursed pouch in his satchel and turns his focus to the approaching dragons. I look more closely at the creepy boxes. "Chloe, come on."

"I don't see the wand or the essence." I sigh.

"Forget it." Tash demands. "We've got to get out of here."

"No. We need Judith to help us free the boys."

"Your life is more important."

"Tash, I'm not a baby anymore. You don't have to protect me all the time. I am capable of," Zenuvius roars again and I forget what I am saying.

"Can we have this conversation later?" Tash is unusually frantic. "I'll come back for it. Come on."

I can't take my eyes off Hagla's spell boxes.

"Stop looking at them," he says, "Close your eyes."

I can't move. A heavy evil feeling is drawing me in like a magnet, like it has control of every cell in my body. It is ominous and dark and strangely comforting.

Zenuvius bursts in through the window. Tash jumps on his back and yanks Zenuvius' head hard to the side pulling him in a circle, riding him like a bucking bronco. Zenuvius shoots bursts of fire back at him and crashes into stone columns furiously trying to knock him off.

The black magic of the charms in Hagla's shrine pulls me deeper into a trance. Time and space seem to cease.

I am in a vision of a moment when I was very young. It is dark except for light shining from under a door. I am being

*held by something, someone, I can't see them, him...he loves
me. I feel comforted. I love him. Heavy footsteps cause a sudden
panic. A single finger presses my lips gently, shhh. I am enveloped
in white light, wrapped in a black shroud and hidden behind
a small door. Someone else is now in the room. I feel a shock
through my heart and intense sadness.*

The vision ends when Zenuvius spins around and hits
Tash with his spiked tail, slamming him into the wall next
to me. It knocks the wind out of him and shocks me back
to reality. He is sprawled on the ground next to his satchel
of arrows. The pouch has fallen out of it. I am about to help
him up when I notice a glowing jar near the center of Hagla's
cabinet.

"The essence."

As soon as I grab it Zenuvius is at my back. I turn
around holding the essence in front of me. I think, when I see
his big nose this time, that we are goners. Zenuvius sniffs me,
but doesn't breath fire.

"You won't destroy this?" I look up at him, holding
the essence between us and help Tash up. I lean him against
the wall, then, while staring Zenuvius in the eye, grab the
satchel and the pouch.

Zenuvius glares at me, waiting for his move.

Outside, dragons hover, guarding every window.

I don't know what to do. I just hold the essence in
front of me and stare back at him.

Tash surprises us by throwing dust from his pocket

into the fire. Sparks light up the room with a flash of bright light. He clutches me tightly to him, covering us both with his shadow and bolts out the window. Before I know it, we are at the bottom of Hagla's deathly valley where Hal is anxiously waiting for us. Tash steps out of his shadow still holding me.

"What happened? Why didn't they see us? Indian magic?" I ask.

"No, a trick that Jayce taught me." He admits.

"Boy, am I glad to be out of there."

"Hal, we found Judith's essence." I say happily.

Tash looks me directly in the eyes. He seems sad.

"You did well," He says quietly, "and you are wrong to think that you don't matter. The whole town cares about you. Even me. Especially me. I care about you, very much."

The way he looks at me feels nice. It isn't the same excited, stomach full of butterflies, feelings that I had in my dreams with Jayce. This is deeper, but different. I hand the pouch and his satchel to him, and then panic.

"Monica's still inside."

"No, I'm not. Do I have the touch or what? The hag was snoring before the mask dried." She steps out from behind Hal with a sleazy grin on her face. She folds up her latex costume and it spins to a tiny size that she places in her purse.

"I have never been happier to hear your whiney voice." I laugh and hug her.

She flicks me off like a dirty bug.

"Pillywiggin, you owe me big time and I will collect."

"Monica, you were fantastic!"

"Yes, I know," she says it like she's bored. "Can we go home now? Seriously, if I don't eat and get at least six hours of beauty sleep I get all puffy." She winks at Tash while twirling a long strand of her hair.

Hagla's yell echoes from the castle. "They tricked me! After them!"

Dragonshrill shakes the boulders around us. Hagla blasts out of the front doors riding Zenuvius. She points her wand at black storm clouds sending them crashing into each other setting off lightning, thunder and rain.

"Zackarack tack twist a dor," she chants.

We are drenched in seconds.

Tash motions for us to move behind him, keeping out of sight. Monica cuts in between us. Tash looks right at her.

"Monica, get behind me," he says urgently.

Monica is shocked.

"You can see her?" I ask.

Tash is focused on Hagla and her dragons. The witch's face mask and hair conditioner are being rinsed off by the downpour.

"Monica, the rain must be washing the fairy dust off you."

"Agh! You're kidding!" she whines wiping the dripping mascara off her cheeks. "He can see me like THIS?" Monica's shrill is like a siren. A crow spots us and caws our hiding spot to the enemy. Hagla and Zenuvius dart for us.

"This is what I was afraid of." Tash says it so angrily.

"HAL, get them OUT OF HERE. NOW!" he yells.

Hal grabs us under each arm.

Tash jumps up shooting, his arrows hitting every mark.

Hal flies quickly swerving around rocks. I struggle to go back, watching for glimpses of Tash.

"Let me go." I scream. I strain to open Hal's claw but he squeezes harder.

Tash is fighting valiantly against insurmountable odds. He is flying so fast he is hard to see. His arrows are hooked to ropes that foul wings, sending crows and dragons crashing to the rocks below.

Hagla zaps black magic at him like a machine gun. He flips out and her blasts destroy boulders where they hit.

The dragons close in on him just as I almost get free to help Tash. He sees me squirming and glares at Hal. The dragons gun for us. Hal swings us around and flies faster. Tash snares Hagla with a rope and swings her high up into the top of the dome. The shock knocks her out and stops the rain. She falls unconscious. Zenuvius flies up to catch her on his back.

Tash watches Hal race up the ridge with us. That was his mistake. Hagla catches him with his own rope. It is my fault. If he wasn't looking to make sure I was safe...he was captured because of me.

Hagla is salivating as she magically reels him in slowly, savoring the moment. He fights hard to get away but it is no use. The dragons surround him flaring fire high into the sky, victorious. They have finally caught the mightiest warrior.

We watch helplessly from the ridge as they shackle his arms and legs and force him to kneel before the witch.

This time I have to hold Hal back.

"There are too many of them," I whisper. I feel so guilty. My mind is racing, trying to think of a solution, anything, to get him out of there. But it is hopeless.

Hagla and Zenuvius close in on him.

"Tashuhunka. You have been a naughty boy, catching and freeing my spies. You thought that would keep her safe, did you?" Hagla milks the moment.

"It worked long enough." Tash glares defiantly.

"So, she is the heir."

Tash laughs.

"You think that is funny?"

"She's just an orphan I found in the woods. Believe me, the protection she needs is from herself. Your spells are unraveling on their own."

"My spells don't unravel." She points her wand at him. "How did you break through the force field?"

"Your truth spell won't work on me. Face it witch, you're going down."

"You first." With a zap of her wand at the ground around him, he is sucked underneath with crinkly black bugs crawling on top of him. I've never seen him so frightened. I have to look away.

Icky and the Black Dragon land next to Hagla.

"Oh no." Hal gasps.

"Two more dragons, so what?"

Hal just watches with desperation.

"Whoa. Madam," The short orange one remarks, "I have never seen your hair so straight and shiny," blatantly sucking up.

"Really?" Hagla primps, pleased with herself.

The black dragon clears it up for me. "Icky and I found a secret tunnel. Tashuhunka has been using it to help the boys."

"Tell her the best part," the little one flutters excitedly. "Wait. Wait. I'll tell her. Hole in the force field at the end of it. Leads OUT. Like we could go to town and get a bagel."

"This changes everything." Hagla sneers sinisterly. This is bad.

"Can we beat them to the tunnel?" I ask Hal. "We can close it up."

"Get on." He says seriously.

We sneak out of the camouflaged hole in the force field that Tash made. I grab the magnets and we jump on Hal's back as the hole shuts behind us.

"I have a purse." Monica holds out her handbag expectantly. I drop the magnets inside.

"Which way is Main Street?" Hal asks.

"Over there." I point.

Before Monica closes the latch, Hal is airborne. Cutting over the forest it takes us less than a minute. We land at the edge of town by Mrs. B's Bakery. I never realized the forcefield was so close on this side. Trees had always blocked it from view I guess.

Magnets that Tash had hung between two trees are still canceling out the electromagnetic charge of the shield here, creating a hole to crawl through. Hal leads us through it and up to the entrance of the tunnel. Ferns that once must have been shielding it are trampled revealing a large rock-crested hole in the ground. Monica is focused on a huge cage that is smashed to bits next to it.

I hop off of Hal.

"You realize that you're insane," Monica cautions, climbing back on Hal.

"Yeah." I give her Judith's essence. "Monica. This is not a face cream. Don't open it. Hal will take you to Judith at the palace. Hurry." I tell Hal. "The elderfairies said she won't last long now without it."

I step toward the tunnel and suddenly realize I have no idea what to do. Hal understands the look.

"Get to Jayce. He is in a cage hanging at the other end of this thing...We had a little trouble," he explains. His eyes get really big. "But be careful," Hal warns. "Hagla's scouts may already be in there. The tunnel ends about two hundred feet above the Shadow Boys cave. Tuck in your wings. Tash usually glides across."

"Across what?"

"Better not to look down. Do not let anyone see you. Well, until you get to Jayce. You can let him see you, of course."

I step toward the tunnel apprehensively.

"Oh, and Chloe," Hal adds with a goofy grin. "Stay downwind from the trolls. They eat just about anything that smells good."

"I smell good?"

"A little like yesterday's ham."

I run back to him and kiss the end of his big nose.

"Will you go already?" Monica complains.

It was like they both know teasing is what I needed. Monica actually cracks a grin, for a split second.

I take a deep breath and enter the tunnel. The inside walls are porous with chunks of rocks nearly blocking the way. After the fifth turn it is pitch black. I fly to the wall and feel my way downward in the darkness. I know I have to hurry. Everyone is counting on me. What I am going to do when I get there I don't want to think about. I just know I am doing the right thing. Whatever it is. I hope somebody has a plan. I am petrified.

CHAPTER 17

A sudden shaking frightens the boys working in the mines. Everyone looks up. "Earthquake!"

Parker rushes out of the Shadow Boys cave and looks around suspiciously. "That was no earthquake."

A rumbling sound, like an approaching freight train builds up as the shaking intensifies and waves of heated air blow into the cavern flaring the hot lava streams.

I am almost to the end of the tunnel. A yellow-orange glow emanates up from below making the walls of the tunnel glisten. It is pretty in a really scary hellish sort of way.

I hear a hissing sound and duck into a crevice just as a slimy snake dragon passes by. I'm about to step out when a second one slithers by, fortunately, looking in the other direction. The third one almost catches me. I press my body into the crevice as far as it will go and hold my breath. The snake dragon passes by me...but, now I'm stuck. It's hot and I'm sweating. I have to exhale practically all the air out of my lungs to pry myself out. I crawl toward a crack in the wall where light is coming from and get my first look at the horrific mines below.

There is a figure in an iron cage just like Hal said. *That must be Jayce.* He's about a hundred yards away from me.

I spot an incredible-looking flying contraption made from petrified wood. Two armed trolls sit comfortably in a copper box that hangs from four thin metal wings. They are sneering at the scene below as three boys peddle hard and fast to keep the thing in the air. It is flying toward me on a path toward the main section of the mine. This is my chance. I can glide above it and use it for cover. I squeeze out of the crack and push off into the air above it. I have to stay in the center of its wings so no one can see me. The air is so hot it stings and my wings are starting to get crispy. Just a little farther, I cringe.

The hanging cage is just ahead. I can't see any trolls so I just hope they are still looking down as I make an aerial dash for the cage. I flap hard to stop before I grab onto it, so it doesn't swing, then tuck my wings back in.

Jayce is lying on the floor in a lump. He watches me approach but doesn't move. Not even after I put my hands on the bars of his cage. He doesn't say anything, he reaches out to brush my fingers from the bars like I am a hallucination. He is stunned when he actually touches my hand.

"Huh!" he gasps.

"Hi."

He sits up, staring at me.

"Jayce?"

He is still too surprised too speak.

"Hal sent me."

"Chloe?" He is astonished. The cavern shakes. "Quick, move to the other side."

The dragon army is approaching the main entrance of the mines. Jayce shields me from their line of sight with his body.

I take the barrette out of my hair and use its clasp to pick the lock. My hair cascades around my face.

"Wow, you are just like in my dreams," he whispers softly.

"You were in my dreams too," I was almost afraid to tell him, but the words came out.

"You mean, it worked? You saw me?"

"Yeah."

I am suddenly embarrassed. I wonder if he had the same dreams I did. The barrette gets stuck inside the lock. Guards are shifting below us, craning their necks to watch the dragons approaching. I concentrate on the lock.

"You actually came." Jayce has the most grateful look on his face. I jiggle the barrette and turn it more gently.

"Tash was captured. Is he here?"

Click. The lock opens.

In a second, Jayce grabs me and leaps to the ledge.

Instantly, a boy flies up to take Jayce's place in the cage, staring at me as he passes.

The roar of dragonshrill echoes through the cavern as Zenuvius leads the mercenary dragon army into the mines. The sound is so loud I feel the vibration pulsing at me.

Jayce and I move quickly down a narrow ledge with boys crowding around us like shields. The looks on their faces is surreal. Each one gasps nearly silently, then in hushed whispers say my name. "Chloe. It's Chloe. Chloe..."

Jayce holds my hand tightly and jumps behind scaffolding in front of the entrance to their cave.

A younger boy runs up to us just inside the cave grinning widely. "Wow." He has such a sparkle in his eyes. "I knew you would come. I'm LB. I sent Hal to talk to you."

Zenuvius distracts us as he lands and stomps to the center of the control level. He stretches his wings and roars fire into the air marking his territory.

Wiggins comes out of the guard station, curious, then, seeing Zenuvius, quickly flutters back inside.

"What's going on?" Cosentino bellows angrily.

"We are taking over." Zenuvius seethes.

"Wiggins give the signal. We're outta here."

"No. Stay," Zenuvius hisses. "You will want to see this."

The mighty dragon takes a commanding stance and flares his flame violently into the air. The other dragons roar in unison.

Cosentino and Wiggins step slowly backwards and duck into the guard station.

Boys everywhere take cover. Those near the cave, hurry inside.

Back inside the Shadow Boys' cave, it is organized chaos. Boys are quickly dressing for battle. When they see me they stare like I am the strangest creature they've ever seen, but continue dressing—without any thought of modesty. They are focused, as if this is a routine they have practiced many times. There is an extreme sense of urgency in the air. They strap weapons under their clothing, wrap digital wristbands on their arms and tuck tiny communicators in their ears.

"This is it guys, move." Jayce leads me through a secret sliding rock door into a hidden cavern. Boys shut the door behind us.

I follow Jayce and LB to the back of the cave where a few boys are looking at computer screens and packing hurriedly.

"I've seen them, before. Wow."

They are stunned when they see me.

"Chloe, this is Parker, Leo, Beav, Max and you met LB. These guys are the best of our best."

"I'm Max." Max offers a gentlemanly handshake.

"Hi." I reach out to shake his hand. He is afraid to touch my hand at first. When he does, he grips too hard.

"Ow."

"Don't break her," Jayce laughs.

Leo's mouth is wide open. Beav socks him in the stomach with a pack. Leo shuts his mouth but keeps staring.

Jayce's demeanor turns serious in an instant and he looks me right in the eyes.

"What happened to Tash?" Jayce's question alarms the others.

"We were leaving Hagla's castle when she caught him

outside. He was sucked underground."

"You escaped the Twisted Castle, and came here? By yourself?" Jayce is astounded.

"Tash was captured?" LB is horrified.

"You know what she'll do to him," Leo worries.

"What?"

Jayce won't tell me. He seems mad when Max does.

"Tash knows stuff the witch wants...bad," Max says.

"Where's Hal?" LB asks worriedly.

"He's fine. Tending to Judith." At least I did one good thing. I feel so guilty about Tash.

"You freed Judith?" LB exclaimed excitedly. "Prophecy one, check."

I turn back to Jayce.

"Judith has her essence back. She can help us." I am so nervous everything is coming out "brightly."

"Magic doesn't work down here," he says.

"Not even her wand?"

"The witch's wand does." LB beams.

"Yeah," Beav grumbles sarcastically, "Maybe if you ask her real nice she'll give it to ya."

"She must have Judith's wand too. Her light power is stronger than Hagla's dark faery magic." I chirp.

"Yeah sure. That's why the witch lost the war." Max says sarcastically.

"The dragons are in the tunnel." LB reports reading text messages on his communicator.

"Blow it." Jayce commands.

"It's our only way out." Max says urgently.

"They'll march on the town."

"We closed the opening in the forcefield. They can't get through it."

"Are you certain they won't find a way out? Didn't think so." Jayce will not accept an argument. "Parker."

"On it." He understands.

Leo hands Parker some small packs.

Jayce takes charge like this is a military unit and the guys follow orders as if they are trained soldiers.

"LB. Tell B unit to initiate the test. If the lower track is an exit, get as many men out as possible. Max, run all the sims again. And find another way into the catacombs."

"The sensors don't have that range," Max argues.

"We're going in. Run it or we'll wing it. LB help him."

"Going in? How do we get out?"

"Max." Jayce's serious glare makes Max shut up.

"On it." He types feverishly on his keyboard. It is obvious that we are in trouble. Jayce leads me into his chamber.

"It's my fault. Tash would be safe if it wasn't for me."

"No. If you want to blame someone, blame the witch." Jayce is matter-of-fact about it. He crouches down and opens a hand carved trunk next to his bed.

"I shouldn't have come." I realize. "You are so prepared. You guys don't need me."

He reaches in to the trunk, pushes a well-worn book and blanket aside and gently picks up an opalescent folded cloth that is tucked neatly under them. He holds it, pausing thoughtfully.

"We waited a long time for you." He admits softly.

That surprises me.

"Tash told us stories about you since we were kids. I don't know how much of it was true...They were good stories. Did he tell you anything about us?"

I want to lie to him. I flash back to what Tash did say. YOU SAVE THEM AND YOU DIE! I know better than to tell Jayce this whole escape thing is not supposed to end well for me. Instead I tell him, "Tash said I wasn't ready."

"You shouldn't have come," Jayce says angrily.

"You think I'll mess it up too?"

"No. No, that's not what I meant."

Unlike Tash, Jayce softens immediately.

"It's not your fight."

"Sure it is. Tash is my friend...and I want to help... you...if I can." I don't know why I feel shy around Jayce.

"There's no way out of here except full blown war. Did he at least train you?"

"For what?" I thought fast about all the things Tash taught me when I was a kid. How to hide mostly. Run away, fly away, get away... great. Toss pencils at oranges so they drop into a basket. I am going to be a HUGE help. I feel my eyes widen to the point of stretching.

Jayce smiles like he thinks I am kidding.

"Oh, okay then." He says it with such a sparkle in his eyes. Then Jayce hands me the fabric he has been holding. It is an outfit.

"You should change...in there."

He points to a slate shower behind a partial rock wall that is about as tall as my shoulders. Now, I think he is kidding.

"We don't have much privacy here. If you want me to, I'll leave."

"What's wrong with the clothes I have on?" The shiny bodysuit he gave me is soft, but....it's a bodysuit.

"Nothing. You look great." He rolls his eyes. "You're hot. I mean, it's hot. It gets hot down here. This material will keep you cool." He blushes.

He turns his back to me as I step into the shower. I take my shoes off, then my dress. I hang it over the wall. "Can I leave my undergarments on?"

"Oh boy...." he sighs.

"What?"

"Yes. Of course." He is trying hard not to turn around to look at me.

"What did Tash say I could do?" I must have sounded nervous because Jayce laughs.

"Don't worry about it. Obviously, he kept secrets from both of us. What is important is the men believe you are the key to our freedom. Now that you're here, they'll fight hard to make it true. What you needed to do, you've already done."

The suit fits like a body stocking with a hood, gloves and clunky insulated boots.

"Does this thing come with superpowers?" I kid, stepping from the barrier.

Jayce laughs, then turns around and freezes when he sees me. His gawking expression doesn't help my overwhelming feeling of self-consciousness as I stand in front of him in the bodyclinging warrior outfit.

"That bad?" I sigh.

"Oh. No." he gasps. "You're perfect. I mean it fits you perfect....perfectly."

He turns me around adjusting it. "LB made the material from compounds here in the mines. He's quite the inventor. This was my first suit. Pull the hood up when you want to go stealth. Then press this button. Magnets shift the crystals. It will reflect what's around you."

"I'll be invisible?

"Almost. It's a little too shiny. Stay close to me. I'll shield you." Jayce notices that the top clasp isn't buttoned. "Here, let me help you with that."

He leans so close I can feel his breath on my cheek. He pushes back my hair then, stares at the birthmark on my neck. His eyes follow it up to my ear, my face, my eyes, my lips... He is more beautiful than in my dreams.

From behind, it must look like he is kissing me. I wish he was.

"Are you kidding me?" Parker enters, interrupting.

Leo is right behind him grinning hopefully. "Can I kiss you too?"

"I was fastening the clasp on her suit." Jayce explains.

"With your face?" Leo says.

Parker is the only one who doesn't laugh.

"What is it?" Jayce's tone snaps back to business.

"There are too many dragons." Parker tells him. "Every way we run it we lose."

Jayce hurries back to their "ops" center. Max and LB work on their laptops with grim expressions. The guys are so focused they don't even look up until Jayce is standing between them. Then they all stare at me.

"LB?"

"Huh? Oh. We bite it bad outside." LB mutters.

"Our best shot is taking her army out down here."

"Tash doesn't have that much time." Jayce sighs.

"What do you mean?" I ask.

"I have a plan." Parker says eagerly. "You take a team to break out Tash and come back for us." He holds up a detonator.

"Lock you guys in with them? No. It's too dangerous."

"Jayce, we can do this." Parker repeats.

Max looks up at me. He has eyes just like Monica.

"The traps are set up for Oddizens, not the dragon army." Jayce reminds him.

"None of us would be alive if it weren't for Tash." Leo said. "Let's go."

Jayce pauses, staring at the detonator in Parker's hand.

"Okay. But don't take any chances. Get everyone to safe zones before you blow it."

"Right." Parker acknowledges. "Bring back some pizza."

Jayce steps back into his room, looking around like it was the last time he'll see it. He goes back to the trunk and quickly stuffs the book and two small pouches into a leather satchel. One last glance and he heads for Leo and Beav.

"B unit's in position," Max reports.

Leo slips his satchel into a cargo pack strapped on Beav's back.

Jayce gives Max a nod. "Cue it up."

Max picks up a headset and pushes a key on a switchboard as he speaks into the mic.

"It's a go." He says firmly.

Jayce changes his earpiece and slides a spare into his belt. Then he places one gently in my ear. He holds my finger to it, showing me how it works.

"Press here. It's a comm line," he says quickly. "Max, patch me in to the men."

Leo, Beav and I walk with Jayce toward the exit. Boys step aside making a path for us to walk through. It is surreal. The expressions on their faces are so serious.

LB unhooks a hand-held computer from his laptop and follows us, slipping it into his backpack.

Someone slides the door open for us.

Max starts a remixed track of Eminem's *Lose Yourself* that he geared up for this battle for their lives. The level is soft, but the beat is driving. Jayce glances at me, then, touches his earpiece as we walk through.

CHAPTER 18

"This is it. Our time is up here." Jayce's tone is haunting over the driving beat of the music.

The boys in the outer cave stop what they are doing as we pass. The surroundings are harsh and Jayce's stride is so brisk it is hard to keep up.

"This is the moment we trained for," Jayce's voice over the com line is strong and inspiring. I can tell by the way the guys watch Jayce they all look up to him—and admire him as their leader.

"From this point on," Jayce says firmly, "we are no longer slaves for the witch. We are FREE MEN."

Meanwhile, on the lowest level of the mines near the bottom of the ravine, hot vapor blasts from the smokestack of a steam engine as it pulls eight titanium train cars into a heavily guarded tunnel. Dragons circle high above them as if they are waiting for something. Only trolls are on this lowest level. The deadly sulfuric steam is yellow and hangs low like fog.

Five boys listen to Jayce via tiny earphones as they

follow Grimly, moving stealthily into a dark tunnel then wait for the train. The boys, wearing breathing devices and protective full-body guard uniforms duck inside their shadows on cue. Grimly shuts his light down and they jump onto sides of the last car. Within seconds they restrain troll guards on each end, shove them inside the car and take their places—listening to every word of Jayce's speech.

"I'm going to level with you. We have nothing to lose." Jayce tells them solemnly. "We are done here..."

We rounded a corner to a cavern where an army of boys split apart for us to walk through. They are just guys, my age, but if they are afraid, they don't show it.

"We are ready for this, and now that Chloe has arrived, as it was written, the odds are on our side. We can win. "

The train slows as it nears a guard station. The boys seem surprised when it stops.

"The dragons found the secret tunnel. They will attack the town." Jayce continues through the com line. "You know the damage they can do."

Troll guards at the lower level checkpoint search under and over the train. One of the boys in B unit spots Cosentino boarding the third car.

"Jayce, Cosentino's bailing," he texts.

Then he sees Strongarm cautiously supervising a load of crates into the front cars while troll guards look out for dragons. Wiggins, wearing a full body suit and helmet runs inside the third car. Strongarm and the guards join him and the train takes off.

We stop at the edge of the Shadow Boys cave, just inside the entrance and Jayce reads the text message on his wristband. He texts back, *"Stay with him"*.

Jayce peers cautiously out at the mines. This is the first time I am able to see the whole ravine. The scene is incredible. Wicked dangerous. Every level of the mines are guarded by Oddizens and Trolls pacing on cracked ledges that are almost too narrow for them. And as if they aren't enough, Hagla's dragon mercs circle the ravine and more are flying in. Ropes and rickety catwalks are the only ways across.

How are we going to get out of here?

I watch boys in the mines sneak into positions as they listen to Jayce on their hidden earphones.

"We've got to lock them in here." He says. "Fight smart. If you can't capture, evade, distract. Do what you can to keep each other alive."

Jayce signals for the boy in the cage to free himself and continues.

"We are no longer simply fighting for our freedom. We are protecting our town, our homes, our families. Our very right to exist," he glares. "Our advantage is that the enemy thinks we are weak. We will show them the men we have become. We are a force they will no longer contain." He pauses then whispers solemnly, "To freedom."

Everywhere, boys whisper back, "To freedom."

He shuts off the com line connection and glances back at us. "Wait here."

Jayce steps off the ledge and falls backwards.

Wha'?

Leo and the others don't seem surprised.

Jayce lands on scaffolding then jumps down on a ledge below in plain sight of Zenuvius. A snakedragon takes a swipe at him from above. Jayce grabs it and holds a knife to its throat. Zenuvius whips around and lands on the ledge next to him. The ground cracks beneath his heavy spiked feet as he stomps aggressively to Jayce. Icky lands next to them with a soft thud. The snakedragon jerks side to side, but Jayce holds it firmly, glaring defiantly at Zenuvius.

"Set us free and I'll let him live." Jayce says fiercely.

Zenuvius impales the snakedragon with his front claw and flicks him off. The snakedragon falls, burning into ash before he hits the lava river.

I feel my knees buckle. I really want to go home.

"The difference between us is obvious." Zenuvius hisses venomously. "You will never defeat me and there is nothing you can give me that I want. Surrender and maybe I will only eat some of you."

Jayce grins charismatically. "What? Give up before the battle?"

"Battle? More like a stir-fry," Icky laughs. "Face it. You and your boys are done. Outnumbered, outsized and soon to be sizzle-ized."

Zenuvius is amused. He leers at Jayce about to say something foreboding, but Jayce beats him to it.

"We are done taking orders from you and your witch."

"Is that right?" Zenuvius scoffs. "And what are you going to do about it… FAIRY?"

Jayce grins slyly, then rolls over the side, out of sight. Seconds later, he reappears "surfing" a skatewing hard and fast directly across the ravine. Zenuvius and Icky race after him. Jayce makes a sharp turn then swerves the other way blocking their dragon flames with the underside of his skatewing. He jumps off and hides behind rocks watching Zenuvius and Icky follow the skatewing. Zenuvius flames it, then swats it into the wall breaking it to bits. He races downward through the pieces searching for Jayce.

Above him, Jayce climbs up the cliff to a ventilation unit. The guards spot him just as he turns a key. Cool air blows in so forcefully it slams Icky to the other side of the ravine. The temperature in the ravine falls fast. With a glance from Jayce, a boy near him blows into a makeshift shell-horn. Its low echoing sound alarms even the dragons.

Leo, LB, Beav and all the Shadow boys on the upper levels jump off the ledges, open their angular wings and glide in unison like stealth bombers in formation. It is an awesome sight, but it turns violent quickly.

They attack in organized aerial combat like a squadron of F-117s. Diving with nets between them, they herd surprised trolls and Oddizens into spring loaded cages they had hidden in scaffolding. Boys on lower levels fight guards with martial arts moves that defy gravity. Their skill and readiness catch the enemy completely by surprise.

Boys on skateboards and tricked out bikes jump the train tracks and twirl into 360's as they launch repeating arrows at the guards. Winged peddlecars manned by three boys each, two to peddle, one at a gun, shoot pointed pebbles from automatic slingshots mounted on their bows.

Above them, their comrades dart around the guards, flipping and spinning, dropping nets, catapulting rocks and gems, and crashing scaffolding to capture or crush the enemy.

I lose sight of Jayce, and there suddenly seem to be less boys fighting.

Parker hides behind a bolder just below the heavily guarded mine entrance. Jayce appears out of nowhere right above him. He, LB, Leo and Beav step out of their shadows and drop nets over surprised guards. Dragons and Oddizens try to escape the nets but tangle themselves more until they fall over the side. Parker leaps up from below and connects a device to wires hidden in the rocks.

Meanwhile, on the other side of the ravine, Zenuvius is up to a dirty trick following the old routine of putting boys in danger to make Jayce give up. He, Icky and the Black Dragon herd boys toward a fiery pit on a hot lower level where Oddizens are standing around the edges with big gnarly clubs. The dragons blow flames at the boys forcing them downward. The air there is getting too hot to fly in. One boy's wings blister and he falls into the pit. His screams get Jayce's attention.

Jayce tucks in his wings and dives onto a skate-wing passing below him. The boy riding it jumps safely onto a ledge then Jayce spins out in a hard turn as a boy from above tosses a spear to him.

More boys are being pushed into the pit. Their wings

burn as they try desperately to stay between the dragon flames.

LB, Leo and Beav jump on to skate-wings and join Jayce, air surfing toward the frantic boys. Guards attack, aiming to knock them off. Jayce uses the spear to flip a dragon backwards. LB shoots arrows clearing a path for them to sail through, then spirals upward landing on a ledge, letting his skate-wing fall. It hits a dragon on the head, sending him crashing onto the rocks below.

Jayce heads for Leo and catches the other end of a thick rope net. They sling it over Zenuvius and push him into scaffolding. Beav throws a rope over him, tying his wings and mouth shut. Zenuvius smashes into the walls trying to free himself. Rocks and scaffolding fall onto guards.

The Black Dragon flies away fast trying to escape a landslide. Peddling a makeshift airplane, Max swoops in from the side and catches the dragon's neck in a noose. Max swerves up and jumps out just before the plane crashes into the side of the cliff. The rope lodges in the rock with the Black Dragon dangling unconsciously from it.

Beav drops a rope ladder down to the boys in the pit. Leo, Max and LB and other boys, fly them to safety on skatewings and peddlecars.

Icky begins untangling Zenuvius when Jayce sneaks up on him. In a twist of his hand, Jayce wraps a leather strap around Icky's neck.

"Do I look like a crow to you?" Icky huffs irritably.

"I'm not going to ride you," Jayce tells him.

Zenuvius snarls at Jayce.

"Are you gonna skewer him too?" Jayce sneers back. "No. This one you care about."

"Mou mul mrgrt dis," Zenuvius mutters angrily trying to scrape the rope around his mouth loose.

"What?" Jayce kids. "Sorry I can't understand. You should do something about that muzzle around your face."

"He said you will regret this," Icky says sharply.

"Oh, I don't know. I'm likin' it already." Jayce looks Zenuvius boldly in the eyes. "As long as we live, he lives." And with a dashing smile he takes off. Jayce flies upward pulling Icky with him. The strap tightens as Icky tries to get it off choking his flame into a fiery burp.

"Go ahead. Struggle." Jayce tells him. "The more you move, the faster you gag."

"Oh sure. Pick on the little guy."

Zenuvius strains at the rope and debris restraining him and tugs his arm lose, then frees his mouth just enough for a flaming roar.

The Black Dragon wakes and shakes himself out of the noose, then races to him anxiously.

Max, in a winged peddlecar with a net on the tail, darts to rescue a boy stuck on scaffolding on a hot lower level.

Jayce joins Beav, Leo and LB behind a train car two levels below. I fly down to join them.

Jayce is mad at me when I get there. He glares at me but doesn't say a word. He gives the end of Icky's rope to Beav.

"Insurance. Muzzle him." Beav ties Icky's mouth shut.

"Hey," Icky doesn't get the whole word out.

Leo straps him to Beav's back in two moves.

Jayce switches my suit to stealth mode making my body almost invisible. Only my head shows clearly.

"Tash didn't train you at all, did he? How could you come down here with no training?"

"Hey, you guys sent for me. What was I supposed to do, say no? I'll be fine."

"You're a distraction. You could get a guy killed."

"I see that. I'm sorry." I mumble guiltily.

"What are you doing?" Leo defends me. "She came all the way here to help us. Don't make her feel bad."

That's when I notice there is something clearly wrong with Jayce. His eyes are dark and his face is pale. The other guys are behind him and don't see.

"Is that the curse?" I whisper.

Jayce doesn't answer. He twists my hair behind me and pulls the hood over my head. The hood fabric is thinner than the rest of the suit. It hangs loose and I can see through it. By the time Jayce finishes he looks normal again.

"I'm sorry. I didn't mean what I said. Stay close to me. If you lose me..." He looks at Leo. Leo grins really wide. "Beav keep an eye on her."

The boys move into their shadows and disappear. It looks like the light is flickering as we fly right over the guards unnoticed. Jayce looks down at the battle scene. The guys are losing. He pulls me into a crevice on the ceiling.

"Why are we stopping?" LB whispers.

Jayce pressed his earphone. "This was a bad idea." Jayce says softly.

Parker hears him through his earphone as he clings to the side of the cliff near the secret tunnel entrance. "Jayce, we've got this."

"It's not working. They're onto our moves already." Jayce says.

"I'm blowing the entrances. Make your choice. In or out." Parker whispers firmly. "Are you gonna get Tash or what?"

Jayce pauses.

"Time's up. I'm blowing it."

Above Parker, dragons loaded with ammunition packs march into the secret tunnel.

"That's not good." Leo understates, nodding up.

"They're carrying explosives." Jayce says urgently. "Parker. Abort. Parker. NOOOOOOO!"

Too late. Parker sets off the first charge. The explosion ignites the dragon army's ammunition. Jayce shields me and Beav shields him, but the shock wave blasts through us. It makes my whole body hurt.

A wave of explosions ripples up the tunnel. Chunks of earth jettison into the caverns crashing down on the dragons and guards inside it. Lava breaks through tiny cracks and sprays into the cavern. A slab of ceiling crashes onto scaffolding sending tools and contraptions flying like weapons in a dense dust cloud. Boys, trolls, dragons, and Oddizens jump for cover as a freight car pummels the cliff face.

LB looks blankly at Jayce. "So what are we doin'?"

The guards spot us. Dust blocks the light the guys need to make shadows.

"There they are." Zenuvius roars flying swiftly from the back of the mines.

Oddizen and dragon guards converge on us. We flip out and scatter, flying fast toward the exit. Max and other boys in flying contraptions pelt rock-based ammo, blocking for us, but some guards make it through and are gaining on us.

"They're not going to make it." Max sighs.

Another explosion blows me sideways, knocking me into Beav. He is so strong it is like hitting a wall. It doesn't even phase him.

Max swerves to avoid falling rock and the peddlecar blades almost hit me. Jayce spins me around just in time.

"Gotcha."

Other boys duck for cover as we bolt toward the exit dodging chunks of earth falling around us. Jayce and Leo pull nets loose above the guard station, then, Beav tackles the bearing post on scaffolding. The scaffolding falls on two guards, but a nail catches LB's backpack and he is stuck.

Zenuvius rages toward him inhaling, readying his flame.

LB's hands are shaking so much he can't get the clasp open. I am the closest to him. Something comes over me. I don't know...a rush. I try to free LB but Zenuvius is closing too fast. Nails that had fallen out of a bucket are scattered around us. I pick one up.

"What are you gonna do with that?" LB asks sarcastically. "Poke him in the eye?"

I grab a few more and race toward Zenuvius head on. He flares his fire as I aim the nail at him like his eyeball is an orange hanging from the tree back home. Bullseye! It hits his eye mid-center and bounces off, but it is enough to distract him. I give him a flying kung fu kick to the side of the head. He spins like a bowling pin.

LB gets himself loose and darts out.

I race after him, dodging guards and falling rocks.

The entrance to the mine is caving in. Zenuvius lunges, and swipes at me with his spiked tail tearing the hood of my suit. I make it out the exit just before the outer wall explodes sealing the mines shut with Zenuvius and the dragon army trapped inside.

The guys are waiting outside the entrance behind a pile of boulders in a larger underground cavern. LB tucks in his wings as he catches his breath. It is hot here, too. I tuck my wings in as I land next to Jayce.

"Chloe, that was really dumb." Jayce looks at me with that glare I'd seen on Tash, pretty much my whole life. I've learned to ignore it.

"Are you kidding? That was incredible. The babe has guts." Leo is amazed.

"Yeah. I thought I was fried for sure." LB says eagerly.

"I would have gone back for him," Jayce offers.

"I was closest."

"Dude it worked out. Chill," Leo grins while looking at my fistful of nails. "That was hilarious."

"I know," LB chatters. "How'd you learn that?"

"Pencils. Tash told me to use them to knock oranges down from the trees."

"Bulls-eye!" He imitated the shot. His laughter was exaggerated by his adrenalin rush, but it was nice to have something to giggle about.

"Beav, take the nails please." Jayce says worriedly. "You're exposed," he examines what is left of my hood.

"Well, we're out of there." I chirp...I'm finding out that I chirp when I'm scared...lovely.

"You think that was dangerous?" Jayce attempts to stretch the ripped neckline of my suit up to my shoulders.

"I've got duct tape," Beav offers grinning.

"We'll just have to trade off hiding her."

"I have no problem with that," Leo smiles.

"She's one of us now. She's earned it." LB says. "Welcome to the Shadow Boys."

"Uh, if you haven't noticed, she's a girl." Beav said.

"She's got our moves...and the outfit." LB gives me a happy wide-eyed once over. He has a wild, glazed look in his eyes. "Looks MUCH better on her."

"LB, calm down." Jayce said. He puts his hands on LB's shoulders. "Calm down. You're okay."

"Yeah. okay...okay. Okay." LB takes a deep breath.

The dragons and guards are trying to break through

from inside the mines. The pounding shakes the ceiling.

"The whole cavern is unstable." Jayce says examining it. He calls on his earphone. "Parker. Max. Come in."

LB texts furiously on his hand-held.

"Signal's blocked," he grumbles.

Jayce stares grimly at the caved-in mine entrance.

I look up. There is a wide, spiraling tunnel above us. I can't see the top of it. We must be a thousand feet down and it is really hot. Too hot to expose our wings.

"Does that lead to the Twisted Castle?"

"Yeah." The pounding from inside the cave picks up pace. "Come on. We've got a short window." Jayce says.

Beav and Leo shoot cables into the rocks above us and pull on them to make sure they are secure. We hook on and begin to climb.

CHAPTER 19

In the night sky high above us, a crow flies over the Heatherworld's Valley of Death toward a buzzing sound that is emanating through tiny air vents of one of the Twisted Castle's windowless towers.

Inside, the tower dungeon is pitch black except for reddish light shining from a torturer's fiery electric rod. Hagla hovers over her victim deliciously. Tashuhunka is in bad shape. He is slumped between two iron posts, fighting pain as a dark faery minion tries futilely to make him talk. Hagla lifts Tash's head back by his hair and waves an Indian charm in his face.

"How can your Indian magic be stronger than mine? What kind of trickery is this?"

Tash smirks at her. Bad move. She slaps his cheek so hard it whips his head to the side.

"Again," she orders viciously.

The torturer pushes the rod onto Tash's back again. He winces but fights the pain. The contents of Tash's satchel are strewn on a table. Hagla studies the items with intrigue, then spots the dark faery charm Tash had taken from her safe.

"Stealing from me?" She shrieks, tucking the pouch in the pocket of her cape. "Nice try."

She smells the tip of one of his arrows then runs it over his cheek.

"Your grandfather was the most powerful Shaman I'd ever encountered. From what I've heard about him, he rarely used magic either. But, you must have been just a baby when your tribe died. How did you learn his secrets?"

Tash just looks straight ahead.

"WHO TAUGHT YOU?" she shouts.

She changes her tactic and waves the torturer off.

"I could make you rich boy," she begins sweetly. "More money than you ever dreamed of and fairy dust free of the inhibition spell. You could do magic any time. You could have everything you want. ANYONE. What do you say we get out of here and have a long conversation over dinner?" Hagla looks at him inquisitively. "Are you the heir to Drescil's power?"

She studies him. The dark faery shakes his head.

"He cannot be. He is the girl's protector. Emperor Drescil never chooses one person for two tasks."

"Then make him talk or take his place," she glares.

Tash stares forward boldly as the torturer resumes, but the pain becomes too much. His body arches in agony and he lets out a bloodcurdling yell. Suddenly he goes quiet.

Hagla sees a spark of hope in his eyes.

"She's here." Hagla smiles sinisterly and pats Tash's

bloody head with her wrinkled hands. "Now we'll see what is more important to you. Your secrets or your girl."

Tash lunges at her, yanking at his chains.

"Protect her now, boy." She cackles as she exits with her cape snapping behind her. The torturer sneers down at Tashuhunka and turns up the charge.

We are about half way up the tunnel when we hear his scream. Even faint, it pierces into us like a dagger.

"Tash." I gasp.

"Stay focused," Jayce says softly. "He's still alive."

Beav and Leo lead the way securing alternating cables for us to climb up. The walls are too hot to touch, even with the protection of the bodysuit. We are essentially walking up the walls by pulling ourselves up the cables. My arms and legs ache, my hands hurt and I am really afraid I am going to fall.

"Just a little farther." Jayce nods. "Go ahead of me, I'll catch you if you lose your grip."

"No. I'll be okay."

"Humor me."

A loud rumbling from below shakes the cavern and the pounding stops cold.

"The dragons broke through," LB gasps.

"Let's move," Jayce says.

The orange glow from below tells us that Zenuvius and his dragon squad are blasting walls of fire at every shadow and crevice. Jayce grabs me and flies upward fast. The scorching air stings our wings when we expose them to fly but we don't have a choice.

We pause at the top. Four very large Oddizens guard the gated entrance to the catacombs. LB uses sensors in his computer to scan for another entrance. He crinkles his nose at Jayce.

"This is the only way in," he says, glancing nervously back down the tunnel.

Jayce nods to Leo and they disappear into their shadows. Within moments two guards fall unconscious. When the other two turn to notice, Jayce and Leo knock them out from behind.

We rush inside. The air temperature is much cooler.

"Hurry, we don't want to get caught in here," Jayce says. His eyes darken and the veins in his hands are pulsating.

"You OK?" Leo asks him.

A holographic blueprint of the castle with infrared heat sensory images of creatures hovers over LB's hand-held.

"Guards are coming," LB whispers.

"Don't touch the walls," Jayce says. "They're booby-trapped."

"You've been here?" Leo asks suspiciously.

Jayce flies ahead, stealthily. Beav shields me in his shadow as we pass over the guards, then rushes upward through the twisting catacombs. They are like a maze.

Jayce chooses a path.

"Wait." LB looks for a more direct path in the blueprint of the castle on his computer. "Oh, that will work."

LB accidentally drops his hand-held.

As soon as it touches the floor, the walls, floor and

ceiling become black. Crinkly black bugs converge on us salivating and chomping their tiny teeth.

"Gross." LB mutters in Jayce's ear.

Bugs fall from the ceiling. The guys stomp at them.

"No, stop." I yelled, as quietly as I could.

"Tash said they might just be under a spell."

CRACCK!

"Too late." Beav grunts worriedly. "Oh no, it's okay he's just limping. Sorry guy."

I crouch down and look one closely in the eyes. It stands still and listens to me. "We do not want to hurt any of you."

I'm not sure if the bug saw me, or his own reflection, in my glasses, but they all stop attacking and crawl back inside the walls.

"Cool" Beav says.

We run into a corridor and stop.

"This is spooky. The castle's empty." LB grumbles.

"Don't let it fool ya." Jayce whispers ominously. "Nothing is as it seems." Anger is building up inside him. He glances around the corner, unsure which way to go.

LB studies the holographic blueprints.

"What about Judith's wand? Can you see it?" I ask LB.

"This thing only picks up body heat." LB tells me. The ground shakes from below. "The dragon squad's haulin'."

"This is insane," Leo complains. "Can we just get Tash and get out of here?"

"What? Do you think I'm making this up?" Jayce

whips his knife out aggressively.

"I didn't mean you were." Leo watches him cautiously.

"Relax," Jayce grins.

Leo is relieved when Jayce presses the knife to Icky's throat, and loosens the muzzle.

"Thanks," Icky says. "That was starting to itch, and I had a million gags I couldn't get out."

"Where is she keeping Tash?" Jayce is all business.

"Where do you think? Your room." Icky grins knowingly. "How are you doing, Jayson? Snapping yet?"

"What's he talking about?" Leo is alarmed at how familiar Icky seems to be with Jayce.

"Hah!" Icky laughs. "You kids are dragon-food. You should start seasoning yourselves now."

"Somebody's coming," LB warns.

Jayce tightens the strap on Icky while looking around suspiciously. Icky tries to flame, but Jayce is too fast with the muzzle. He nods up and we jump to the ceiling. The guys slip into their shadows and cover me.

Four Oddizen guards pass under us tapping the walls suspiciously with spears. One almost hits me.

The curse starts to affect Jayce, again. After an intense moment, he regains control of himself and his eyes and skin go back to normal. As soon as they are out of sight Jayce, drops down.

"He'll be in the north tower," Jayce says with reluctance.

"How do you know all this?" Leo asks suspiciously.

"I have been here before."

The veins in his neck and hands swell up and then subside.

"Because of me, huh?" LB says solemnly.

"Come on, we're wasting time." Jayce scowls. He is obviously fighting a surge of unexplained anger.

"What's with you?" Beav asks.

"It's the curse." When I said it, I thought they all knew.

"What curse?" Leo asks, surprised.

Jayce walks faster. Leo cuts him off. "What curse?" Leo demands.

"It's nothing." Jayce says firmly, and calmer than before.

"Spill." Leo demands.

Jayce is hesitant to answer, but he does. "The witch hexed me when I was a kid."

"And you're telling us, NOW?" Beav blurts.

"I didn't tell you because, it's nothing. I can control it. Don't worry."

Jayce turns his head toward the sound of a low wind. A quick glance back at us and the guys instantly tuck in their wings and we hide among the shadows on the walls.

The dragon squad storms into the hall, seconds later. Zenuvius catches a glimpse of candlelight reflecting in my bodysuit. Jayce presses me up against the wall, shielding me inside his shadow. Zenuvius examines the wall next to us, closely. I hold my breath. Jayce catches my stare and doesn't flinch.

"Don't tell me you missed them?" Hagla snarls after she materializes next to Zenuvius. Her voice makes Jayce cringe.

"There's no sign of them. Maybe they didn't get in," the Black Dragon growls.

"They are here," Zenuvius hisses, coincidentally leaning up inches from us.

His scalding breath on Jayce's back make him arch and press his body harder into mine.

"They can hide inside their shadows."

"Really?" Hagla coos. "Jayson, I am impressed." She can't see us, but glares down the hall with an eerie smirk trying to distract us so we'll slip up.

"You learned that from the journal you took from me?" She seethes sweetly. "Very good. Jayson, you have come far this time. I thought you would never attempt another escape after what happened last time. It is time to give up now, dearie. You know intruders do not survive inside the Twisted Castle."

She stops to listen for the slightest sound.

"You want to play?" She holds Jayce's cursed pouch up for him to see. "Remember this?" She looks up and down the hall for signs of us.

"Ahh, you have learned to control the spell. Excellent." she says with a sinister grin. "Controllum Jaysonem expellous nominous rom. Now try that one." She cackles.

The look in Jayce's eyes is suddenly wild. Then he

focuses, on my face and presses harder into me like he is trying to control a dark urge inside him.

After a long moment the witch gives up.

"Well, we know where they're headed. Lightaski Queas. Let's see how far they get now."

The guys take a worried expression from Jayce as a cue and duck around the corner.

Jayce carries me and we make it out of the hall just as the lights shut off. He lets go of me and we fly up the stairs. The guys haven't used their wings this much before, and are getting tired.

CHAPTER 20

With a few levels behind us we slow down. The witch and her dragons aren't following. In fact, it is quiet. We all know what that means.

"Jayce, you realize we're walking into a trap?" LB warns.

"Yes."

"So...Do you have a plan?"

"I'm thinking."

The twisted stairwell did the same dirty tricks as the first time I climbed it, giving us hallucinations to deter us.

"Uh, how's that plan coming?" LB asks quietly.

Jayce tries to hide it, but he is getting more anxious the higher we climb.

The wallpaper swirls in a dizzying pattern. Beav sways and his cheeks puff out.

"He's gonna hurl." LB whispers harshly.

Leo jumps ahead, out of range.

"Close your eyes," Jayce whispers.

Jayce takes Beav's hand and leads him up the stairs.

We reach a level with several elegantly furnished bedrooms.

Beav opens his eyes again, feeling better.

"Thanks. I'm okay."

We hurry carefully across the hall to another set of stairs. Leo stops in a doorway and is gawking at a luxurious canopy bed.

"Guest rooms? How wicked would a dude have to be to actually want to sleep here?"

"Let's not find out," Jayce recommends, and we move on.

A few floors below the top level, the game changes. The walls in the stairwell actually close in on us like a pulsating funnel, forcing us to land single file and tuck in our wings.

Beav has to crouch. He strains to hold the ceiling up to let us pass. Jayce rips a brass candlestick light off the wall and twists the exposed wires together creating an electric arc. He shoves it into the wall. The walls grind to a halt.

Unfortunately, just as Beav lets go of the ceiling a gooey substance similar to rubber cement seeps over the steps making our feet stick. There isn't enough room to spread our wings, and more goo is flowing in by the second.

"Oh, yuck." LB grimaces.

"Run." Jayce whispers urgently.

We run as lightly as we can to stay on top of it, but the higher up we climb the thicker the goo gets. The last flight of stairs is the worst.

"Agh. I'm stuck." LB can't move and he is blocking the

way. Beav pulls up on him.

"The legs don't come off." LB kids. "At least I hope they don't."

Leo springs off Beav, does a somersault and lands at the top, looking down at us...pretty full of himself.

Not to be outdone, Jayce flips into a triple spiral and lands beside Leo.

Beav throws LB at Jayce and Leo. They catch him and set him down, upside-down.

"Hey!"

They laugh and flip him to his feet.

Of course, being a few steps below, I see all this from between Beav's legs. Up until now I hadn't really processed how actually huge the boy is. He is like the biggest bouncer I've ever seen. An incredibly massive muscular wall of guy—and he is carrying a dragon on his back. Beav turns sideways and looks at me while the guys wait expectantly.

Oh sure, a triple flip up the stairs without using my wings, no prob. Granted, there is a little room to do it, but, I am embarrassed. They are so good... and I'm not that good.

"Do you want me to throw ya?" Beav asks politely.

"I think I can do it."

My foot is stuck. I flip upward and hit the wall, instinctively reaching out for help. Beav catches my hand and then falls backward toward me in what seems like slow motion. I don't know who is more horrified, me, Beav or the dragon.

Oh, the thud.

It must have looked pretty bad from above. After he hit, Beav doesn't move. The guys are silent.

Leo's question is muffled, "Is she dead?"

I take that as a cue to breathe.

"No, I'm good." I wheeze.

Beav had braced and rolled, thank goodness, and landed just beside me. His body still pushing me down, but at least the whole weight of the big guy didn't crushed me.

Somebody throws a tapestry onto the stairs. I can't see a thing. My face is pinned between Beav's chest and forearm.

Somebody's laughing?

"Icky fainted," Jayce chuckles. He and Leo crawl onto Beav and unhook the dragon.

"Wimp," Leo chortles and carries Icky on his shoulders to the top of the stairs.

Beav tries to find somewhere to put his knee.

"Ugh. Not there."

He pries himself up and crawls to the top level.

"I can't move." My entire body is glued down.

"Are you hurt?" Jayce asks sincerely.

"Aside from my ego?"

LB throws Jayce a tapestry banner. He places it on the steps next to me and lays on it, looking me eye to eye.

"You couldn't have thought of using the tapestry thing before?"

"What, and miss this?" He grins.

Why is it that whenever I am this close to a really cute guy my backside is usually stuck in something?

Jayce tries to pull me up. "Leo. A little help." he groans.

Great. Leo and Jayce pull on me so hard they start sweating. Sweating. Here. Nothing like making a girl feel feminine.

"Guys, I really don't want to lose the back of my suit."

Finally, a change in tactic and wedging their hands between my body and the rubbery substance to breaks the suction. The goo pulls off like rubber cement but only a few inches at a time.

"Why are we still alive?" Beav asks. "The hag can see us, right?"

"She's messing with us," Jayce says. "Think of yourself as entertainment."

Beav sighs.

"As long as she's focused on us, she's not on Tash," Jayce whispers.

A flash of dark blue changes the color of Jayce's eyes and his skin lightens showing the veins in his face. He clenches his fists in a flush of anger.

"Are you okay?" I ask.

Leo looks at him seriously.

"It's getting hard to control," Jayce whispers so only Leo and I can hear.

Above us, LB taps his earphone.

"Max. Parker. Anybody there?" He presses keys on his hand-held worriedly. "It's like they disappeared."

"The cave's been open since the dragon's broke out," Leo said. "We should be getting a signal."

"Uh-oh. Four big ones coming this way." LB warns.

Jayce begins to sign in the language of Tash's ancient tribe. Something Tash taught me as well.

"I will pretend the curse has a hold on me. That will get me into the tower. I'll send you back a scan."

"I'll go with you," I sign.

Jayce doesn't argue like Tash would have. Instead he signs to Leo, *"If I lose it, do not hesitate to take me out."*

"30 seconds," LB whispers.

"We're going as fast as we can!" Jayce says heatedly in English. "This isn't easy. She is built like a brick house."

"Great, now I feel feminine."

"Hey, I'm just sayin' it's gonna get a lot harder in twenty, nineteen..." LB counts down.

"I wish we had more time, this is the most fun I've had my whole life." Leo grins.

Jayce glares at him with pitch black eyes.

LB catches a glimpse.

"It's the curse," he gasps.

"Beav," Leo shouts.

Beav pulls us all up like we are weightless.

Jayce and Leo let go of me and tumble into a heated fight. Jayce punches Leo in the jaw, spinning him around.

"What are you doin'?" LB exclaims.

The guards are running now. Heavy footsteps and clanging metal echoes off the stone walls. Leo bounces back and comes at Jayce full force with a sweeping kick and double punch that catches Jayce by surprise. He flips out of it and kicks Leo in the back, knocking him to the ground, then shoves him down hard, with his foot. It looks real to me.

"Jayce! Stop. You're hurting him." I plead.

LB and Beav disappear into their shadows. Beav reaches for me but Jayce grabs me first, around the neck, like a prisoner.

The guards are on us in an instant. One of them, a tall Zulu looking Oddizen with a thick ponytail that stands straight up and bones of dead animals pierced all around his neck, puts a spear to Leo's back.

"Bring him," Jayce orders them. He bends my arm behind my back and pushes me up the stairs to the north tower.

When we reach the door to the north tower, Jayce opens it slowly. The hinges creak ominously. The room is dark. A buzzing red light illuminates the face of the torturer. He looks at me with a sleazy grin on his face, and then moves the light to show Tash slumped between two posts. His bare chest and legs are bloody and bruised.

A white light flashes in the room and the dark faery's head snaps to one side. He crumbles to the floor. When the light fades Jayce is standing angrily over him, totally blowing his cover.

"So much for faking it," Leo quips sarcastically.

The witch and six of her most fierce dragons hover on the ceiling, above a sheet of flames. We duck and roll for cover under a metal table as the fire blazes around us. The Oddizens aren't so lucky. They fry.

The Zulu Oddizen skewers the dragon that flamed him at close range. The dragon's fire burns them both to a crisp.

Jayce and Leo use the distraction and the shadows to climb up the walls and surprise the dragons from above. Jayce hurls a chain around the neck of one and Leo pulls it back and locks it to the wall. The dragon flails so violently he knocks himself out.

I run toward Tash but a sheet of fire chases me, lighting torches all around the room. I knock the metal torture table on its side and crouch behind it.

Jayce jumps out of his shadow to help me. Zenuvius and the Black dragon lock their tails together and slam him and Leo into the wall. In seconds, we have all been caught.

Hagla floats down gracefully. She is seething with a sickly horrible vibe.

"Did your friends enjoy your tour?" Hagla's cackle echoes off the rock walls. "Come now Jayson. Join us and let's get this over with."

"Let us walk out of here, all of us, and we will not harm you." Jayce says determinedly.

"Darling, everyone you care about is dead. Well, except these two but we can remedy that."

Hagla slithers close to Jayce and studies the changes in his appearance. His skin is so pale some of his veins show through it and his eyes are now a dark shade of blue.

"It is getting difficult to fight the spell isn't it? Ah, is it painful?" She smiles.

"I can fight it. Turns out you aren't that powerful."

"Surely, you are not going to fight me and the best of my dragon army by yourself," the witch laughs.

"No, but I will blow up Zenuvius' favorite jester," Jayce says coldly. Zenuvius glares at him angrily.

"You're bluffing," Hagla sneers. "It's not in you to kill an innocent."

Jayce presses his communicator sending a text message that reads, NOW. A second later, an explosion from the level below shakes the tower. Shadows shift.

"He wasn't that innocent." Jayce glares.

Zenuvius rages fire at Jayce and in doing so, lifts his tail enough that Jayce and Leo can slip out. They flip backwards and disappear into their shadows again. A moment later Jayce opens the tower door. He glances at the witch and is gone.

A feverish darkness sweeps over the room.

Jayce, Leo, LB and Beav seem to fly out of nowhere as they attack. Leo snaps the end of a chain, tripping twin dragons while Beav whips another chain around their necks.

Hagla blasts magic from her wand flinging torture instruments and balls of fire at us. Jayce beats them away using a metal tray like a shield.

I make it to Tash and gently lift his head. There are streams of blood down one side of his face and his skin is ice cold. I cut his arms loose and he falls on me with his whole body weight.

Zenuvius leaps at Beav with his claws extended and rips Icky out of the harness. The Black Dragon slams Beav into the wall. LB flips through them swinging a metal spear.

Hagla zaps a chain around his foot and sends him dangling above the twin dragons' flames. LB chucks the spear so hard it sticks both their necks into the stone wall.

"ENOUGH!" Jayce shouts at the witch. "You have taken everything from us. It ends now."

He lunges at her. The witch flicks her wand at him with a devilish gaze in her eyes and slams him into the walls, again and again, mercilessly. He fights to control the spell but is losing.

"Give into the anger Jayson. That's it."

He strains to get away, but finally, his arched body relaxes as he succumbs. She pulls him toward her magically, studying her prize. He hovers meekly under her spell, inches from her.

"Life on this side of the light is much more fun, you will see."

Without changing his expression, he snatches her wand right out of her hand and turns it on her. Unfortunately, nothing happens.

"No one but a creature of the dark can wield the power within my wand," she hisses in an ungodly voice.

She whispers in ancient Gaelic and touches the spell pouch on her necklace. Jayce's eyes glaze over. The hex has him for real this time.

I have to do something.

I lay Tash down gently, then leap up and grab the wand from his hand. A strange sensation sweeps through me. I know very little about magic wands. I am more surprised than the witch when magic blasts from it. Of course, it would have been better if I'd aimed.

A power ball shoots from the wand bending the bar they have LB, unconsciously hanging from.

"Impossible!" Hagla nearly gags.

I point the wand at Hagla as if I know what I am doing.

"KILL HER!" The witch screeches.

Jayce's head whips around and he strikes me. Leo pummels into him, knocking him back. They fight fiercely, but know each other's moves. They spin and flip over one another, moving out of the way just seconds before the other one's fist misses their head and hits the walls. The dragons are crawling on the ceiling, frenzied and salivating for the loser.

Jayce finally hits Leo so hard he spins backwards and slices his shoulder on a metal torture rod. Leo surprises Jayce with a crosscheck. Jayce turns around and punches him right in the chin, then, they collide violently. Jayce is completely under the dark faery spell. The fight is brutal. This is not going to last long.

I reach out for Jayce, thinking I can, help, I guess. He spins around and nearly cuts me with a blade in his boot. Leo pushes me back and hooks Jayce in a leg lock.

"Stay out of this." Leo warns. He loses his grip and Jayce throws him into the wall.

I know I have to do something before they kill each other. I leap at Hagla and try to grab the dark faery charm but I miss. It swings behind the witch. She pulls Judith's wand from her pocket and blasts me. I hold up Hagla's wand, thinking, *NO!* Black magic shoots out of the dark wand. It almost knocks me backwards.

"How can you do that?" She screams. She blasts me into the wall with a golden ball from Judith's wand. It gives me such an adrenaline rush. It doesn't hurt me. I bounce back.

"Get her!" Hagla yells.

The dragons attack me claws out. I spin my wrist in a circle thinking, *NO!* The wand power freezes them in the air.

I bolt at Hagla and yank the chain from her neck. The cursed pouch splits open and a hair falls out of it with an ultraviolet spray of ground black gems. When it hits the floor, so does Jayce.

Hagla glances at him and I grab both wands. We struggle, face to face. She is so evil. I hang on with all my might. I know if I lose, she will kill all of us.

She blasts me with light magic from Judith's wand. It reflects off my suit and hits her in the stomach.

"Aghh!" She cringes.

I am gripping the wands with all my strength. Hagla pulls them back and pricks me with her ring. I try to twist them away, hard. She pulls back, throwing me over her head. I lower my grip so she thinks I lost them, then snatch them away in a somersault over her head. She crashes into the wall and

THE WANDS BREAK IN HALF!

I am horrified.

Dark and light energy shoot out in a flat circle just above our heads blowing off the top of the tower in an earth-shaking sonic boom. The energy continues, cutting the tops off the other towers and jetting out over the horizon.

I've ruined everything. The forcefield is gone. The guys look dead and blood is pooling under Jayce.

Hagla is ecstatic.

"HA! Unbelievable! Chloe Pillywiggin. In one day you solved all my problems. It is unfortunate you were pricked with my ring, I could have used a disaster-prone ally like you."

My fingers are turning black.

"Oh, that little plague thing you have now is deadly." Hagla laughs and turns to Zenuvius. "Blow up the mines. We're going to town! HA!"

She cackles gleefully all the way up into the sky, free of the dome at last.

Zenuvius lets out a resounding dragonshrill and leads the dragons into the catacombs. Hagla darts to her lab.

"No," I gasp. "It can't end this way."

I feel woozy and lose balance. A discoloring plague starts to creep up my legs like a scaly bluish crust. It is draining the energy from me.

I am not sure if the guys are alive. I don't know who to go to first. Leo is lying on the ground next to me. I put my hand on his neck. His vein is pulsing, and he is breathing.

Okay, good, I think.

I am afraid to check Jayce. Blood is spewing out from underneath him. I crawl to him and turn him over. I am so relieved to see that he is just lying on a torn dragon claw. It isn't his blood. I touch his face and he opens his eyes.

"Are you okay?" I ask him.

He sits up.

"Am I okay?" he laughs teasingly. "How did you do that? You used her wand like a pro."

"No, I messed up."

He sees my blackened fingers and is alarmed. "What's this?"

"Nevermind." I point to the pieces of the broken wands. I am fighting back tears. "She got away."

"It's okay. We live to fight again," he smiles softly.

Jayce helps me up and looks around. Tash is lying unconscious between the posts, LB dangles unconsciously from the bent rod and Beav is lying under a table snoring.

"Tash." As I step toward him, my body gives out.

Jayce catches me. "What did she do to you?"

"The old handy ring stab, thing, ugh." I feel awful. Something inside me is trying to come up.

Jayce examines my finger where her ring cut me. The plague is making its way up my torso.

"I am so sorry," I apologize, "Tash was right. I made everything worse. But, please don't wake him up until after I'm dead, I don't want to hear him say I told you so."

"What? No. Chloe. You're going to be fine."

"Right," I sigh sarcastically. I feel like I am going to cough but I can't get enough air. "It's okay. My destiny. The prophecies said I that didn't survive this."

Jayce is shocked at this tidbit. He stares at me for a moment, and then says, "Don't give in."

He is so serious it hits me as funny.

"Change your fate," he says.

"You mean like, the power is within me?"

"Yes."

"Do you know where, exactly?" My laugh turns into a very weak cough. Suddenly it isn't funny anymore.

Jayce looks at me so sweetly while he holds me gently in his arms. "Chloe, stay with me."

I don't want to go. I want him to hold me forever. I feel like I am sinking inside my body. The plague has crept up my neck and is starting to cover my face. I feel myself drifting.

"Chloe. Don't go." Jayce holds me tightly. "I can't lose you." He looks frantic. Then his expression changes. He looks deep in thought.

He presses his lips to my ear. I feel warmth. *Was it words? Did Jayce say something?* I suddenly feel a little stronger.

Leo wakes up just in time to see Jayce kiss me.

What timing. Something clammy and horrid is stuck in my throat. I roll over hurl up a slimy black lump.

Leo thinks it's the funniest thing he's ever seen.

"UGH! Dude you made her gag." Leo cracks up.

Great. Now he'll never kiss me again.

The plague is gone–or on the floor–disgusting. Jayce leans over to look at it. I try to stop him.

"You don't want to see that."

He looks. His jaw drops on the double-take. Jayce jumps up to get away from it and knocks into LB.

"You wanna get me down from here?" LB huffs.

Beav climbs out from under the table and groans at the sight of the black lugey. "Agh! What is that?"

I do feel better. Maybe the worst is over.

I cut Tash's legs free not paying attention really. I am avoiding the truth. I cradle him in my lap and try to wipe the blood off of his face. After a moment I realize my tears are washing it away.

Tash is lifeless. Jayce touches him then drops to his knees beside me. Tears stream down his face.

"He's dead."

"No." I try to revive him. The guys rush over.

"Tash is dead?" LB gasps.

They kneel around him solemnly, not believing it at first. But the proof is undeniable. Their mightiest warrior is gone. His body is empty and cold. I wrap my arms around him and rock him, hoping he will wake up.

Beav looks up at the starry pre-dawn sky. One by one the other guys notice it. This is the first time they've seen the sky since they were taken.

Sunshine peeking up from the horizon begins to warm our faces while tears make rivers in the dirt and soot on our cheeks.

The roar of Hagla's dragons organizing above the ridge draws our attention. The tower sways side to side, like rolling thunder as the rest of her army swarms up from the base of the Twisted Castle with wicked frenzy.

We lay down pretending to be dead as the army of dragons whisks over us wearing ammo packs on their backs.

Armed Oddizens follow in flying contraptions that are peddled by trolls...no boys are in sight.

Earthquakes shake the ground and stone remnants of the tower walls break away in chunks. Hagla rides Zenuvius mightily in front of her dragon army as they line up ready for battle.

"This is the day we've been waiting for! We'll take our revenge on Penstemon and then march on to Fairydom. It is our time to rule the realms!"

They roar violently when a faint dust cloud rises up from the valley. Then, they head off toward Penstemon en force.

Jayce stands up like he is going to chase after them by himself. Suddenly, the ground above the mines cracks and thousands of feet of earth and rock cave in on itself. There is absolutely no way that anyone caught under that massive, crushing force could have survived.

Jayce involuntarily sits down. The castle tower sways side to side, almost to the point of breaking off.

I don't know how long we stared at the destruction. I vaguely remember Hagla and her army disappearing into the woods, focused on Penstemon. I am still holding Tash when my shock wears off. I caress his face, hoping to wake him up.

The guys don't have any fight left in them. They are devastated.

Then, Jayce's demeanor switches and I understand completely why they had made him their leader.

"Chloe, you should wait here, at least until you get your strength back." Jayce says calmly.

"Where are we going?" LB mutters.

"To save the town."

"Jayce, there are four of us."

"Five." I tell them.

"I was hoping you'd say that." Jayce smiles.

Jayce kneels beside me and tries to take Tash. "You have to let him go."

LB stares at a GPS image on his hand-held. "They haven't attacked yet. What are they waiting for?" LB whispers.

The hologram image shows Hagla's army is silently creeping in on Penstemon, from all sides, but not attacking.

"Maximum impact." Jayce says. "LB, do you think you can sneak past them and warn the town?"

"Yeah. No problem." He starts to leave.

"Hey," Jayce says softly. "It's probably better not to tell them what happened here. Not yet."

"I understand." LB ducks into his shadow and slithers over the side of the tower.

Jayce gingerly starts to pull Tash out of my arms. I don't want to let go.

"Chloe."

I let them take him. Jayce and Leo strap Tash's body to Beav's back and we leave.

We fly low over the Valley of Death, cautious for scouts or stray crows then, sneak up on to the ridge. We are hesitant to see the damage the witch's dragons had done, but they still haven't attacked. They are waiting...with such sinister intensity it electrifies the air.

"We need weapons." Jayce whispers solemnly.

CHAPTER 21

LB approaches Penstemon Palace from the far side of town where the line up of dragons is less dense. It is eerily still, but the dragons are amped, waiting readily for the order to attack. Hiding within his shadow LB slips around the muscular legs of two dragons and sweeps up into a palace window like flickering light.

The scene inside is rushed and urgent. Palace guards are arming themselves and organizing. Fairies are rushing around urgently as if they already know. It catches LB off guard. He stands next to the window and watches. A maiden spots him. Her gasp draws everyone's attention.

"A boy!" Someone says with complete shock. Then someone else shouts, "A boy!" Hushed, shocked whispers about the boy, pass through the crowd.

LB just stands there staring back at them, somewhat in shock himself. Prince Peter pushes through the crowd and gently takes his hand.

"It's all right," he smiles. "Come with me."

He is unsure but he goes with him. The crowd parts

for them, smiling at LB as he walks past. He starts to feel braver until the chubby little king runs up to him as if his life depends on it.

The king tries to speak but is too excited and finds himself out of breath. Queen Rose steps regally from behind the king.

"We were just coming to get you. I am truly sorry that so much time has passed," she says apologetically.

"We know," LB says calmly. "The spells made you forget."

"What is your name?" She asks.

"LB."

"Where are the others? Are they with you?"

"Coming, but, the dragon army has surrounded the town. The witch is going to attack."

"You heard him," the king shouts. "Get ready! Everyone."

The crowd scurries back into action, organizing and arming themselves.

"I don't understand. Hagla is able to escape the dome? What happened to the spells?" The queen asks.

"Chloe broke the wands."

"Wands?" Peter asks quietly.

"Judith and Hagla's...light and dark wands."

Peter tries to hide his interest, but asks, "How did she do that?"

"She said it was an accident. I didn't see it happen actually." LB said meekly, "I was unconscious."

"Is she all right?" Queen Rose asks.

"That's what I'm saying. She's gonna attack."

"No, I mean Chloe."

"Uh, yeah. Actually, I should get back."

"Honey, no. You are safe now. You'll stay here. Ursula, please get him something to eat."

LB is unaccustomed to genuine maternal type concern and it makes him uncomfortable. Besides, it is not the time for a snack. The queen flits into an adjacent room. LB breaks through the guards and follows her in.

"No. You don't get it. You guys are gonna get creamed. Do you have any magic you can use? Where's Judith? Is Hal still here?" LB senses the danger mounting by the second.

The king rushes in and the guards grab LB by the arms. "Go with them son, it will be all right."

"No," LB yells determinedly.

The guards lead him and Peter out of the room as the king and queen stay behind speaking secretively in heated whispers.

Peter looks around to see if anyone is watching him before he rushes upstairs.

LB breaks away and loses the guards in the crowd. Then, hiding inside his shadow, he doubles back. He makes it inside the library just before the doors close. The royals are arguing in whispers.

"...but, Judith is not well enough yet. We have no other choice," the queen says strongly. LB has to move out of the way quickly when the king walks right toward him.

The king tips over a table lamp and flips a switch underneath it. The walls become electrified nearly singing LB. He hides in the shadows of a bookcase and listens to the royal argument.

"Rose, the moment you use your power they will know you are alive, and where you are," the king said worriedly. "Think of your children," the king pleaded. "All that you have done and sacrificed for Peter and Chloe will be lost."

"They may have found me already," Rose says softly.

"What do you mean?"

"Peter."

"He would never disclose…"

"I don't think he's Peter," Rose says solemnly.

"No." The king is shocked. "You think he's a replacement?"

"I hope I'm wrong. He seems too perfect."

"Well, if that's all it is, Peter has been raised at the best boarding school in Europe."

"Maybe." The queen notices an extra shadow behind the king and nonchalantly walks toward it. "Have all the fairy dust brought to the courtyard. We will do a protection spell. Bring everyone inside."

The queen grabs LB and drags him into the light.

"How much did you hear?" The king demands.

"More than he should have," the queen says, looking at him seriously.

"I'm sorry. I'm sorry. I, just uh," LB is used to being in

trouble, so he thinks fast. He decides to ignore the question, focusing on the solution to the problem, like Jayce taught him. They are about to be slaughtered by the witch and her dragon army yet something scares the queen more.

"I promise I won't say anything," LB says cautiously."

The queen shuts off the electromagnetic field.

"Guards."

Palace guards rush in. LB wriggles out of the queen's grasp and evades the guards by flying up the walls and across the ceiling in his shadow. The queen flies up to grab him just as LB slips to the open window.

"I will keep your secret," he promises her, "Put your shield up though. We'll be attacking from the forest."

LB disappears. Four guards chase after him and are captured by dragons.

Meanwhile, we've landed deep in the woods where Tash had made his home. "This is, was..."

Jayce finishes my sentence for me. "Tash's camp," he says solemnly. "It looks the same."

"You've been here?"

"No. He used it to teach me how to dreamwalk." He picks up a king from a handcarved chess set. "He beat me at chess so many times I accused him of cheating." He sets the king back down and looks around thoughtfully.

Leo and Beav study the camp silently. I lay a blanket on the soft grass and they set Tash's body on it.

I hear a faint thumping when I pick up a wooden bowl and fill it with water, but don't think much of it. I kneel next to Tash and begin to clean the blood off him.

"Chloe, there isn't time." Jayce says. "Where are the weapons?"

"There. Pull on that vine."

When Jayce pulls it, something leaps out of the trunk and attacks him. It moves so fast it is hard to see what it is. They roll over and over struggling. Jayce finally gets a grip on it and stands up triumphantly, holding it upside down by its boot.

"What is it?" Leo asks.

"I am not sure," Jayce says staring at it.

"It is a gnome." I tell them. I read about them in one of Tip's books. "At least I think it is."

One of its legs is black like a bug. The gnome must be at least three hundred years old and he is really mad.

"Well, you sir are an idiot. PUT ME DOWN!" He yells in a raspy voice with a Scottish accent. "THIEVES! THIEVES!"

"We are not thieves," I say.

"Oh, Chloe. I didn't see you." He slips out of his boot and is standing next to me in an instant.

"You know me?"

The guys are staring at him as if he is the strangest thing they'd ever seen.

"After all you've been through, you think he's strange? That's funny."

"Would you be so kind to give me back me boot sir."

"That's a gnome?" Beav asks with amazement.

The gnome jerks his boot from Jayce and puts it on, then notices Tash lying on the blanket.

"Why is he sleeping?" he asks me.

"He's not sleeping, he's dead." Jayce says sternly.

The gnome rolls his eyes at Jayce.

"He's not dead?" I ask the gnome hopefully.

"No sweetheart."

"She's a sweetheart and I'm an idiot?" Jayce huffs.

"That's right." The gnome gives me a wink and shakes his bug leg. "Residue."

"You were a bug, under a spell? The wands broke."

"Is that what happened?" He says. "Come on, now. Gather round me. We've got to break the trance before his soul travels too far away." He nudges Tash and gets nervous. "I do hope we are not too late."

The guys kneel around Tash.

"Do as I do," the gnome tells us. He places his hands on Tash's head and begins to hum a chant I had heard Tash do many times before.

"He's just dreamwalking?" Jayce is surprised.

"Something like that." The gnome says with concern. He gives up. "The lad is too weak."

"Try. Please." Jayce pleads.

We place our hands on Tash's body, close our eyes and chant softly with him.

A brisk wind sends the terrifying sound of Dragonshrill and screams through the forest.

"They're attacking." Beav says urgently.

Jayce turns impatiently to the gnome. "Can you speed

this up?" Jayce orders.

"Not if you don't focus," the gnome grumbles.

"We'll focus," Jayce says.

"Not them, you."

I hear myself say *I'll get the medicine charm* and then realize I am out of my body.

"You don't need that," Tash says, "I'm here."

"You're all right?" I gasp.

"Of course," he smiles.

I try to hug him and go right through him.

"We don't have time for this." Jayce is dreamwalking with us but is not in the best mood. "The witch is attacking the town and if you haven't noticed, you're fading."

Tash looks at himself. He has little time left to get back into his body. Tash notices Leo, Beav and the gnome. "You mean we did it? Everyone's free?"

Jayce and I look at each other, neither wanting to say it out loud.

"The others?" Tash asks.

"Dead." Jayce's anger jerks him out of the vision.

I am instantly aware of my body again. Tash is being ripped from my grasp by Jayce. He throws Tash to the ground like he is a rag doll.

"Jayce, stop. He's not even conscious." I plead.

"Wake up." Jayce seethes.

He picks Tash up and rams him into the tree Tash had rigged as a shower. Water dumps onto them knocking them both down. Tash coughs. Jayce pulls him up onto his feet and then punches Tash hard in the jaw. Beav stops Jayce's next punch with his open hand.

"That's enough." Beav says firmly.

Jayce twists out of his grip and relaxes for a second. His fist comes out of nowhere, shocking Tash with a punch in the face so hard it knocks him to the ground.

"Don't EVER lie to me again."

Leo helps him up. Tash adjusts his jaw. Jayce is fuming.

"What's done is done," Beav tell him. "Cool off."

He shoves Jayce under the shower and dumps water on him until Jayce succumbs.

"Okay. Beav. Stop."

Beav finally lets up.

"Are you all right?" I ask Tash.

"Yeah."

Jayce takes off his boots and pours the water out of them.

"Chloe, the weapons," He says it like it is an order. Then he glares at Tash. "You do remember me telling you the witch is attacking the town?"

Tash walks off.

"Oh that's it, leave. Go sulk somewhere."

"He isn't the enemy," I remind Jayce.

I go to the secret hole in the ground where Tash hides his arrows and look for everything we can use as weapons. Jayce cools down a bit and helps me.

The sound and air movement of dragon wings in

unison brushes through the trees as waves of wind. It is ominous.

Jayce looks back at Leo and Beav who are about one comment away from an emotional freak out explosion themselves.

"That water felt good." Jayce admits.

Leo tries out the shower. Beav shoves him out of the way and takes his spot. Leo shoves back and they both fall.

"Ugh. Man. Beav, get off me." Leo blurts in a muffled voice from beneath Beav.

"If you ladies are done dancing you can come get some of this gear." Jayce teases.

I just finish outfitting the guys and myself with feathered Indian charms, arrows, knives and small hatchets from the underground chest, when Tash returns, carrying much better stuff. He laughs and tosses a gnarly looking spear and shield to Leo. The guys drop the chachis and we grab gear from Tash. Jayce holds back apprehensively.

"Do you have something for me?"

"That depends. Are you going to use it on me or the dragons?" Tash smirks.

"Not sure yet." Jayce lightens up.

Tash hugs him. Jayce is really glad to have him back.

"Now who's dancing?" Beav asks.

Tash hears a rustling and almost kills LB.

"It's me! It's me. Hey, Tash, you're alive." LB is so happy that he jumps on him. "What'd I miss? Who's this guy?" LB leans inches from the gnome's face examining him curiously.

"It's a gnome." Leo deadpans.

"Gnomes don't exist," LB says in a hushed whisper.

The gnome leers him.

"Boo."

LB jumps back.

"Hi, LB, glad you got back okay." I say as I hand him some water.

He stares at me thoughtfully.

"Are you okay?" I ask.

"Yeah." He takes the water. "Thanks."

Tash nods to some gear leaning on a tree trunk and starts to leave. Then he notices my warrior suit.

"She looks great doesn't she?" Jayce grins.

Tash picks up the blanket and to wrap me in.

"It's a little late for that," I laugh.

Jayce grabs his gear.

"It's obvious why you kept her for yourself." he taunts

"I didn't. She wasn't ready." Tash defends.

Jayce passes him, following the others. "Oh, she's ready," he grins.

Tash doesn't know what to make of that comment.

"You should have seen her take out Zenuvius with a poke in the eye!" LB exclaims passing by him with arms full of gear.

Tash looks at me, momentarily in shock, and all I can do is grin and blush. Then leave really fast. After a few seconds he catches up to us and leads us cautiously through the forest.

CHAPTER 22

Screams tells us Hagla's army is already on the move. We stop about a few hundred yards outside the village, behind enemy lines. Tash lifts a rock to find a magical key and uses it to open the door of a tree. LB is delighted.

"Wow. Do they just leave those things lying around?"

"You have to know where to look. Go inside," Tash whispers.

LB excitedly steps inside. The gnome is waiting for us with a lantern at the bottom of the steps.

"Who is this guy?" Jayce asked.

"Not too quick is he?" The gnome says to Tash.

Tash glances at Jayce and smiles at the gnome. Then he takes off, running briskly down the tunnel. We all follow. I am glad there aren't any more bugs to not step on. I catch up to him first, but the gnome passes me carrying the lantern. Tash stops next to another set of steps.

"We're in the middle of town, by the school. Head right. Take cover where you find it. Chloe stay here with Pugsley."

"Spell wore off, I have two legs now," Pugsley says.

"Pugsley, thank you, but no." I smile at him. "I'll go with you guys." I tell Tash matter- of-factly.

"We do not have time to argue. He'll take you to the next county with the others."

"Why doesn't Pugsley go get the others so they can come back here and help us fight?"

"That's a good idea," Tash says with surprise. "Pugsley, do you think they will fight with us?"

"The witch had us all spellbound in darkness and dirt eatin' unimaginables. What do you think?" Pugsley responds with a drawl.

"They want revenge?"

"Nah, a pint is more like it. They'll not be comin' back here. That is for certain."

Tash stares at me, thinking.

"Chloe's one of us. She can handle it," Jayce says firmly.

That is really nice to hear.

"All right, but stay close," Tash succumbs.

He climbs up to the ground level and opens the door in the tree trunk, just a crack.

Fire blasts from outside. Tash quickly pulls the door shut and listens. After a moment he opens it again. The fire has passed. Tash waves us out. We exit and hide nearby. It is chaos. Panic in the street. Cottages are in flames. Fairies have turned fire hoses on a squad of dragons who are swirling aggressively crushing and destroying what is left of their homes.

Professors Boone and Higglewitz join Pops, Mrs. B and other townspeople in the street. They are armed with garden tools and are ready to use them.

The dragons howl, laughing and snorting, then one swats the tree pruner out of Pop's hands and they attack. Mrs. B and Professor Higglewitz turn their leaf blowers on them. All it does is puff up the dragons cheeks and make their lips flap.

Hal races in between them, flying in front of the townspeople protectively.

"Get to the palace," Hal says bravely.

Royal guards rush over and escort the fairies up the street. A bull dragon takes the blower from Higglewitz and blows her dress up as she flies away screaming.

The dragon squad turns their wrath on the storefronts breaking windows and burning flower carts, but lets the fairies go mostly unharmed.

Queen Rose rushes outside the palace gates when she sees fairybabies and toddlers holding hands, flying and walking together as they were taught to do in a fire drill. Monica, Tip and Darling run out to help the Queen hurry them all inside safely.

"Hagla is only scaring them." I think out loud.

The rest of her mercenary army is hovering between buildings, just below the rooftops. "Why are they holding back?" Leo whispers.

Just then Hagla rises over the treetops riding Zenuvius with the Black Dragon and Icky at her side. Her cape snaps sharply as she flies over Main Street with the dragons wearing heavy packs galloping through the air behind her.

"This looks bad," Beav grumbles. "What are they carrying, bombs?"

"It's okay. The royals have loads of dust. They are gonna do a spell to protect everyone in the palace." LB says excitedly.

Gunfire and loud blasts of magic from the palace draw our attention. Eight dragons carry four trunks of fairy dust from the tower screeching wildly as guards shoot at them futilely. The bullets don't even dent the dragon scales.

"You mean that dust?" Beav groans.

The dragons shield their path and they land on the rooftop of Penstemon Academy. Hagla hastens her pace.

"Whats' the plan?" LB asks hurriedly.

"I'm thinking." Jayce and Tash say it at the same time, both believing that they are the leader. It dawns on me that they have no clue what to do.

"There's got to be something we can do! We can't just stand here and watch."

"Even if we take out the squad with the ammo," Leo said pessimistically, "we are way outnumbered."

"Our only shot is to get the witch," Tash says bravely.

"And Zenuvius and the Black dragon," Jayce says grimly.

"Well at least it will be a short fight." LB tries to joke.

We move slowly. We are definitely apprehensive. What we are doing is suicide. Our hope is to make enough of a difference so that at least some of the townspeople will survive this. We amp ourselves up and are starting toward town when Jayce stops.

"Wait," Jayce says urgently.

He is staring at the horizon, searching it for something. He notices a flickering under the dragons. He taps his earphone three times. I heard two taps back in mine.

"They're here," Jayce says with major relief. "They made it. The guys are hiding in the shadows of the dragons."

CHAPTER 23

"Parker?" Jayce whispers.

The response came back as a text message.

You know it.

WE'RE HERE...Max.

LB's communicator lights up with text messages.

"They're here. All of 'em," he grins with a huge sigh of relief.

I look back at Hagla. She has a wicked gleam in her eyes as she nears the palace.

"Hold position," Jayce orders. "Who is closest? Find out what the dragons are carrying."

The dragons hold their arms over the clasps on their packs, ready to open them. One dragon unhooks the clasp early and blackened fairydust sifts out. His wing breaks where the dust touches it.

"Stop." Jayce says urgently. "She's cursed it."

The Black Dragon rips the pack off the dragon's back and lets him fall. A shadow dashes away safely just before the dragon hits the ground.

"On three. Let's finish this."

The boys hear Jayce's order. In an instant, they dart from under the dragons and harness their heads to their necks, trying to force them to the ground. It only works on a few. Dragons buck and tear the harnesses off.

The boys change tactic and fly invisibly inside their shadows attacking like F-18s in a heated dogfight.

Jayce and Tash shield me in their shadows and we fly together after Hagla. Dragons block for her blindly, not able to see their attackers, but her team gets through. We are unable to reach them in time.

The wranglers ride their black crows in from the far side of the forest, heroically, spinning lassos above them with eyes on the enemy.

The two dragons release the dust from their packs on target. The Black Dragon waits for the wranglers and good fairies to fly over the center of the courtyard, then drops the cursed fairydust on them. Their wings break instantly, some tearing as they try to fly.

The wranglers catch several falling fairies, only to have their own wings tear. They crash on top of each other in the courtyard below.

A breeze carries some of the dust with it. Boys and dragons nearest the palace slam into each other as it hits them. A tiny bit grazes me and tears the edge of my right wing.

"You're hit." Tash says urgently.

"I'm okay."

"You're sure?" Jayce asks.

"Yeah."

The guys split off and the fight escalates. They swoop in swiftly like eagles with each dive precise. Tash shoots arrows with expanding nets into the sky. Jayce and LB lock the tips of their spears together to trip the enemy and spin them out of control. Dragons are caught in the nets and tumble into each other, blasting fire aimlessly unable to see their prey.

The witch flies to the roof of the school. A dark faery minion scurries about, quickly removing the trunks of stolen fairy dust from the dragon's backs.

Around me, the boys shred the sky with sonic booms, jetting in and out of mach speed, trying to ensnare the dragon's wings and claws. I am knocked out of the sky. It is accidental, I can't see the guys either, but the impact spreads some dust residue and scrapes my wing more, making it harder to fly.

I use my shield to float downward but a dragon smashes it with its horned tail as it is knocked to the ground by a direct hit from two boys.

I land in the middle of Main Street just as two massive dragons collide in full flame and smash into the side of the school. An explosion blows out the windows of the second floor and the building starts to burn.

"The elderfairies!" I gasp.

I tuck in my wings and run as fast as I can toward the school. Zenuvius sees me and dives at me claws out. I throw my spear at him, but it just sticks in one of his scales like a toothpick. He brushes it aside. I know I am not going to outrun him and there is nowhere to hide.

I see a 6-foot tree pruner lying in the street and run to pick it up. I hold it like a spear, and then turn to face him. I must look like an idiot. The thing has a blunt tip and a pretty yellow rope that is used to pull the pruner open, but the opening is even too small to clip his toenails. I think I might shove it down his throat and then run like heck while he gags, but as he gets closer to me I realize that is a pretty bad idea.

I aim the pruner for his eye, but he catches it in his teeth and bites the stick in half. Suddenly, his head jerks up. Jayce has snared Zenuvius' horns with a whip. Then he jumps on his back and rides him like a bucking bull trying to snag his wings in a net.

When Beav, LB and Leo drop in to help, I make my way toward the school to help the elderfairies escape the fire. Another explosion shakes the ground. The buildings on both sides of the street are in flames.

Clouds are forming above us quickly, blocking the sun. Hagla is chanting from the roof of the school and tossing blackened fairydust into the air to create a massive storm. The sky turns dark. Without shadows, the boys can be seen. Dragons attack with vigor, quickly taking control of the fight.

Tash fights valiantly against eight dragons that are trying to burn the injured people inside the palace walls. He shoots an arrow tied to a net past their line then beats it to the other side tangling the dragons in it.

Pebble-sized hail stings like rubber bullets as it falls around us. A funnel cloud forms above the pond and spins toward us. It touches down, hitting the town as a full-blown tornado. Buildings in its path disintegrate on contact.

I stop to look for Jayce. Zenuvius rams into the Black Dragon on purpose to knock Jayce off his back then swats him toward it.

"JAYCE!" I scream.

The wind carries him around the side of the funnel. I can faintly see him fighting the swift current and using his shield against swirling debris trying to get free. After a moment, he relaxes and places the shield under his feet. He flows with the wind like it is a rip tide then rides it like a giant wave careful not to get too close to the center of the funnel.

He shoots out of it at the Black Dragon, kicking him so hard in the side of the head that his own tongue hits him in the eye. He falls from the sky unconscious and slobbering as he is sucked inside the tornado meant for Jayce. LB and Leo copy his moves, surfing the forces of nature to accelerate their power and fight the enemy with aerial acrobatics. It is dangerous, but gives them the edge they need in the fight.

The tornado pauses just outside the palace, spinning in place and growing with every bit of debris sucked into its grasp. The guys get away from it just in time. The dragons they are fighting are not so lucky. Everyone scatters down the street, holding on to whatever they can as they rush to escape the clutching wind.

Hagla is on the roof of the school chanting beneath an electrified cloud. A thin funnel touches down and swirls blackened fairy dust up inside it. In seconds an ultraviolet ray beams into the sky like a spotlight.

I hurry around to the side of the school and start to open a window. Zenuvius charges at me from around the corner. The window is stuck.

"Come on." I grunt, like talking to the window is going to help.

There is nothing nearby to throw at him and nowhere to hide. I just keep fumbling with the window. It finally opens up about half way, but Zenuvius is almost within flaming range. I get one leg inside and look back just in time to see him get knocked away by an invisible force.

Hal is flying inside the shadows of three boys. The rival enemies engage in battle ferociously like wild animals competing for a kill. LB, Parker and Max watch Hal fight Zenuvius with pride.

"He's waited a long time for this," LB says intensely.

"Zenuvius should hang it up," Max adds. "Hal's gonna put his butt in a skewer."

"It's good to see you guys," I say.

"Good to be seen," Max says dramatically.

"You'd better stay down," Parker warns me.

They disappear in their shadows and rejoin the battle.

I crawl inside. The ceiling is covered in smoke so I creep low to the ground as I run down the hall to the library.

"Why aren't the sprinklers on?" I wonder looking around, when a pounding sound catches my attention. Following the sound I find the book pinned under a fallen shelf. Hagla's spell had broken but the elderfairies are still trapped inside. I manage to free the book and it pushes open. Dark faeries fly out first. I trip one with a mid-air sweeping kick that I'd seen Jayce do, but he tumbles out of it and comes after me. Elsie knocks him out cold with a chicken cage.

"Hmmphff," she huffs.

The other grabs her by the neck and begins to suck the life out of her. She is shriveling from the inside out.

Eunice screams and ducks back inside the book.

I jump on the dark faery's back and try to twist him away from Elsie. He knocks into a cabinet and lets go of her.

Eldon climbs out of the book. He holds his spinning pendulum and creats a circle of light the dark faery cannot penetrate. For some reason, I can't either.

"Chloe, quickly, get inside the circle."

When I run into it the force shocks me back.

The dark faery glares at me, surprised then, attacks, snarling at me viciously.

I throw books at him and then point the school flag at him like a spear. He screams at me in a harsh raspy echo peering into me with his dark creepy eyes. My body starts to vibrate.

Tash leaps through the fiery doorway and attacks the dark faery fiercely, pulling him off of me. Tash hits him with such force the creature spins into evaporating ash squealing eerily until there is nothing left of it.

I drop the flag.

Eldon looks at me like he has seen a ghost. He is

terrified...of me. Then he goes back inside the book. When I reach to pick it up it snaps shut. I look to Tash for an answer.

"What's wrong with me? Why couldn't I get in?"

"I don't know."

The fire is spreading.

"Will you get the elderfairies to safety?" I ask, handing him the book.

"So you can go after the witch by yourself? Not on your life."

I open a window.

"Please. I need you to believe in me."

"I do," he says softly. "But I'm coming. Besides, no where is safe until we win this."

Hagla's wild chanting rings over the town. Black rain begins to seep from the clouds covering everything it touches with thick paralyzing tar. Everyone scurries to get away from it, even the dragon army, but most are frozen in their tracks like screaming gooey black statues. A dragon's flames ignite the tar around him.

Jayce jumps through the window and joins us.

"Don't tell me this stuff's flammable."

The remaining dragons are lining up on the horizon, just above the clouds.

"She's going to torch it?" Tash doesn't want to believe it. He looks at all the boys stuck motionless in the thick tar.

Hal and Zenuvius slam violently into the outside wall of the building shaking several bricks loose. LB dangles at the end of a rope he had thrown around Zenuvius' neck, hanging on for dear life. The black rain is beginning to weigh him down. Unintentionally, Zenuvius flicks his head sharply at the right moment and LB is flung through the window. He crashes on the other side of the room in a pile of books and chards of glass. Jayce races over.

"Ouch." LB moans.

Jayce moves him to a chair next to the open window, which at that point, is the farthest from the fire.

The fight outside between Hal and Zenuvius escalates with another slam to the wall that shakes the building but when they tumble to the ground they stick. They are both pretty miffed about it. Zenuvius blows fire in Hal's face.

"That's all you got?" Hal smirks. "Your breath smells like cat food."

A net drops over Zenuvius from above. Leo and Beav are gliding under billboard signs they had rigged into makeshift hangliders. Leo jumps onto Zenuvius' back, and lets his glider crash beside them. Beav lands right behind him, shielding him from the black rain. Leo quickly cinches the net together, tying Zenuvius' wings down and muzzles his face.

"You okay Hal?"

"De-vine. Mudbaths normally cost a bundle."

Zenuvius makes a last attempt to buck and knocks Leo to the ground. Beav punches Zenuvius in the side of the head and the dragon falls unconscious with a goofy look on his face.

"Oh, where's a camera when you need one?" Hal quips.

Leo's feet and hands are stuck.

"Hang on buddy," Beav says jumping down.

He pulls Leo up with one arm and carries him like a football, but after a few steps it becomes hard to walk. He throws the billboard at the building and carries him farther, pushing ahead with all of his strength. Jayce and Tash pick up the sign and they hold it as a shield from the rain but Beav is out too far. Beav fights hard against the tar, but eventually his legs stick. He can't go on. With a glance to Jayce and Tash he throws Leo. Unfortunately, he aim is off and Leo hits his head on the wall. He is knocked out cold. Jayce and Tash catch him before he falls in the tar and I help to pull him inside.

The tar is piling up on Beav. I look at my arms and the black rain hasn't touched me. Jayce and Tash had new rain drops of tar on them. I didn't have any drops on me at all.

"Beav." Jayce throws the billboard to him. "Cover yourself. At least it won't get any worse."

"Yeah, now I'll feel it when they knock me on the head and burn me." Beav motions to a squad of dangerous-looking armed Oddizens marching from the forest. The black rain dissolves when it touches them.

"The tar doesn't affect creatures of the dark." Jayce says.

My heart sinks.

We can see the rest of the dragon squad above us descending through the clouds, but staying above the black rain. Icky is the last to fall in line. In unison, they shoot dragonfire into the tar drops igniting it into tiny explosions.

"Not too fast," Icky reminds the dragons. "She wants them to see it coming."

We are freaking, to put it mildly. Even Tash. The building is burning and we can't go outside. I look up at the sprinklers.

"The water main is destroyed." Tash tells me.

The dragons blast fire into the clouds until the clouds explode sending a sheet of fire rumbling toward the town. Everyone else is stuck in the tar. No one wants to say it out loud, but it looks like the battle is over, and we lost. I know it is up to me. I have to stop the witch.

"Beav," Jayce calls out to him, "Can you reach into your pack?" Beav tries but almost loses the shield.

"Stop. Nevermind." He turns to Tash, "The book's in there."

"What? You can't be thinking of using black magic."

"What choice do we have?"

Just then Jayce's satchel hits him in the back and lands on the floor with a thud. He looks out the window. Beav is covered in tar, nearly motionless. He had dropped the sign and taken his pack off.

"I'm cool," is the last thing he can say.

Jayce takes a lightly dusted black gem from his satchel and grips it tightly with a gloved hand.

"Get ready to fly. I'll create a protective ice shield that won't melt. We need to be above it." he warns.

Purple energy shoots from the black gem. He holds

it toward the sky and waves it back and forth. The black rain freezes as it falls. Ice crystals form a shield just above the tar, protecting everyone from fire while allowing an air space for them to breathe. The dragon squad darts downward. Tash races up to stop them from reaching the tar. He attacks violently with nets and snares attached to arrows as fast as he can.

"Where's Chloe?" Jayce asks LB urgently.

My torn wings had worked just enough to help me climb up the side of the building before anyone could try to talk me out of it. I am just below the roof line when I take a breath and realize how scared I am.

Jayce leans out the window and sees me from below. "No."

He climbs outside and starts to fly up but a second ice layer forms above him.

"No. Stop."

He tries to chip it away but as he does the gem falls into the tar and sinks.

He ducks back inside and runs to the stairwell pushing flaming boards to the side. The fire and smoke are too heavy. Just as he turns to go back the ceiling below him collapses.

"Jayce!" He hear LB yell.

"I'm okay," he calls back.

Jayce looks around. Fire is all around him, but he keeps calm. He notices the shadows and disappears inside them. The heat is scalding, but Jayce navigates his way upward staying in the dark shadows of the burning room.

I peek over the edge of the roof. I don't know what I am going to do. I have to shut down her spell somehow.

Fairy dust floats from the open trunks into the sky. The witch takes a black gem from a small pack and tosses it into the fairy dust. Brilliant ultraviolet light shoots up like a spotlight.

I run as fast as I can shutting the five trunks. She doesn't see me until the last one shuts. She is shocked. She must have been in a trance. I wish I had known that, I could have done something smarter.

"How can you still be alive?" she cackles angrily.

"What happened to you, to make you so evil?"

That question throws her. She pauses, and looks at me really weird. Thoughtfully, as if she has a tragic story, something or someone has hurt her in her past. But then her expression turns cold.

"Kill her."

I hadn't seen the dark faery minion. It holds a blade to my neck. Then, suddenly it drops to the ground. Jayce is standing behind me.

Hagla opens a trunk and holds a black gem over the light aiming a beam toward us. As the beam moves it burns everything it touches.

I leap at her but she moves out of the way and slams me into the pile of blackened fairydust. The black gem falls into my hand. It feels warm, but my skin is not even pink where I touch it.

"You're not burned?" Hagla gasps with surprise. "WHO ARE YOU?"

The dragons hear her scream but Tash is keeping them too busy to help her. Three fall out of the sky leaving only a snake dragon and Icky left.

A second dark faery minion zaps Jayce from behind with a torture rod. After a second Jayce falls to the ground.

I stand up but she throws another blast at me that knocks me into the satellite dish. My wing gets stuck.

Hagla creeps toward me slowly with glowing black magic circling in a sphere between her hands. I rip my wing but dart out of the way just in time. The blast knocks a hole in the building all the way to the ground. The witch glows and floats upward powerfully, watching me writhe in pain.

I crawl toward her looking helpless, with the biggest saddest eyes I can pull off, slyly snaring the television cable with my foot. Then I turn my bloody wing toward her so she can get the full view. As she gawks at my agony, I spring up and hogtie her upside-down like an owl.

She screams eerily and the black dust is drawn to her like metallic flakes to a magnet. Magically the dust frees her from the cable and swings it back at me tying me by the legs and neck sideways on the satellite dish.

Hagla chants wildly. Black vampire bats gather inside the beam. I throw the black gem at the back of her head.

With the bat of an eyelash she flings it back at me surrounded by spinning circular saw blades. Jayce comes from nowhere and yanks the dish off its brackets then spins me behind him like a frisbee. He takes the hit that was meant for me. I helplessly watch in horror as the blades slice his wings off before the magic gem knocks him off the roof.

"NOOO!" I cry.

But Jayce is calm. He tucks in the remnants of his wings and falls silently, spinning a black gem slowly between his gloved fingertips. After a long moment he is standing on the ledge of the building glaring at the witch. He recreated his wings with magic from black gems. They are ultraviolet and shimmering with black veins and markings. He is partially clean, like the tar was washed off or dissolved in spots, like when it hits a creature of the dark. It is then that I notice the dark minion with the broken neck.

I struggle to get free from the black magic but it is no use. Then I think, *RELEASE ME*, and it does. I don't know which creeps me out more...being captured by the black magic or being able to control it.

Hagla hovers in a magical cloud in front of Jayce, cackling at her devilish handiwork. She blows blackened fairy dust into the air and the ice melts swiftly.

"So what?" Jayce laughs. "Your dragons are history."

Hagla releases the bats.

Jayce raises his hands and tries to recreate the ice.

"You will have to do better than that, Jayson."

People and creatures below are screaming and ducking lower into the tar. Tash lands beside Jayce with Icky in a harness.

"Thank you Tashuhunka, you brought him just in time." Hagla sneers at Jayce. "And you said my dragons were history."

"Icky's dragonfire is more like a hot burp."

Hagla throws a gem in Icky's mouth. He swallows and blows the largest flame anyone has ever seen.

"Now that's what I'm talkin' about!" Icky exclaims.

Tash shuts his mouth with a leather tie just as Icky blows another. The flame comes out his other end in a smoky fart.

"Ohhh, now that's deadly." Jayce quips.

Leo and LB fly past frantically being chased by a group of frenzied vampire bats.

I scoop a black gem in a handful of blackened fairy dust and think, *STOP*. The bats stop, mid-air. Hagla glares at me like she is going to rip my heart out.

She blasts a black wave of magic at me—normally this kind of thing will pretty much make you explode into oblivion—but I can stop it with my mind. I shape its molecules into a spiral and spin it upward until it evaporates. Something inside tells me not to use any more black magic. I pretend to. I cup my hands as if I am forming a ball. The witch starts chanting. Jayce and Tash don't move. She speeds around them with magic swirling around her. I pull my hands apart, drawing her attention, then Jayce walks to her without flinching and punches her HARD in the face. Her eyes roll back in her head and she drops to the ground, OUT COLD.

I think, *STOP*, as I slam the lid on the trunk of blackened fairydust shutting down its power. The bats disappear. The tar all over the town, vanishes. The sun breaks through the clouds. It is over. Finally.

LB and Leo land next to Hagla.

"Wow. I can't believe I was afraid of that." LB remarks.

Jayce's eyes are filled with so much anger and hate. I fear that he might do something he will regret. He stares at Hagla coldly, clenching the dusted black gem tightly in his fist. I wrap my hand around his.

"She's not worth it."

He finally relaxes his grip. He drops the gem, then ties her up like a roasting pig and muzzles her face with the rest of the television cable.

CHAPTER 24

Jayce and I stand quietly on the roof and look out at the now still battlefield. The last of the witch's mercenary army have succumbed.

Zenuvius flails angrily under a net as several boys, Hal and wranglers secure him to the ground.

The sky is clearing and the now neutralized magic powder cascades harmlessly around us like opalescent microscopic snow.

Tash sees the dead minion and turned to Jayce. "Did you have to kill him?"

"Yes."

Tash notices my bloody wing. "You're hurt."

He picks me up in his arms worriedly.

"I can take her," Jayce offers firmly.

"I've got her," Tash says.

He flies us quickly to the palace. Jayce grabs the end of the television cable and drags Hagla under him, knocking her into every obstacle he can as he follows us. Below us in the streets, parents find their long lost sons and sisters are reunited with their brothers.

Tash lands in the palace courtyard and sets me down between LB, Leo and Beav. Jayce drops Hagla ten feet above the ground then lands beside us. She is still unconscious as palace guards shove her inside a prison cart and lock the door.

LB ducks behind Jayce as Queen Rose rushes over to glare at the witch. The king catches up to her panting heavily. Prince Peter waits in a doorway out of sight, watching as if he doesn't want to be seen.

As RSS agents materialize around the Hagla's cage, Prince Peter ducks back into the castle. The agents are dressed in the standard issue blue suit, narrow tie and non-descript haircut. All business. Four agents point handheld devices that scan the perimeter with green iridescent light waves. When the beam hits the crowd a small Oddizen disguised in elderfairy robes, pops out screaming as if the light hurts him. Two agents dematerialize with him as another takes the key to the prison cart from the captain of the palace guards. The remaining RSS agents ready the prison cart for transport.

The guys crow around the captured witch. They are still so angry.

Judith joins Queen Rose just as Hagla wakes up.

"See honey, like I told you, good always wins." Judith coos smiling sweetly. "Bye-bye."

RSS agents shoot a laser at the prison cart, zapping Hagla to who knows where for a very long time. Her shocked expression is priceless. We watch until every last bit of her has vanished. LB runs a scan just to be sure.

"She's gone," he sighs with relief.

The last RSS agents nod a silent salute to the King. He nods back knowingly. They turn to Queen Rose, "Your majesty."

Prince Peter waits for them to dematerialize before enthusiastically joining the group.

The guys are ecstatic. I take my first relaxed breath in what seems like forever and then realize Tash hasn't been around this many people–ever. The crowd is closing in on us. Families are reuniting for the first time in years.

The king and queen and Peter thank everyone while party decorations and buffet tables of food appear in the courtyard. Some of the wranglers grab fiddles and join the band.

Pops picks LB up and swings him around in his arms as Tip watches ecstatically. It turns out he is Tip's brother. LB was the tag inside his LLBean shirt when he was taken. It got torn and only read LB. Pops doesn't tell him what his birth name was. LB fits.

Max finds Monica. "Hey sis," he says nonchalantly. She squeezes him tightly, suddenly realizing how much she had missed him. Leo's dad, the palace guard captain, jumps off a tower to hug him. Beav and Parker's families surround us, all chattering at once, very proud of their sons. Tash looks really uncomfortable. I expect him to leave any second. Then he looks at me strangely. We both sense something is weird.

"Oh, hello." Professor Boone sings as she taps LB with her wand cleaning him up and changing his outfit. "Queen

Rose gave me carte blanche to do makeovers at will."

"Chloe, may I?" Professor Boone asks. I've never seen her so happy.

"You are hurt." A voice behind me says. By the expressions on everyone's faces I guess it is the Queen. She touches my shoulder gently and turns me around. I have never been this close to the Queen. She is lovely, but it is the warmth in her eyes that transfixes me.

"Judith," she says. I hadn't noticed Judith and Hal standing beside Queen Rose until I am spun around in a swirl of Judith's magic. After a moment, my wounds are healed, I am in a beautiful dress and I smell a lot better.

"Exquisite." Professor Boone gasps.

She dances off looking for more fashion victims.

"Are you okay?" Tash huffs at me. He looks great in his new clothes, well, except for his expression.

"Yes. Are you?"

"You look pretty." Jayce says.

Tash gives him a dirty look.

"I meant Chloe," Jayce laughs.

I feel instantly shy.

King Kenneth walks over so brightly his belly giggles with each step. Peter walks beside him hiding a small bag of jelly rolls in his jacket sleeve for the king to munch from.

"What you have done is a miracle," he says joyfully taking a bite. "The Royal Secret Service has taken Hagla and her army into custody. She will be locked in her own dungeon under triple guard."

"The RSS has a special program for her army," the queen adds brightly, catching Peter off guard. He quickly stash away the bag. She continues, "many can be rehabilitated. Those that will not change will be sent to a very nice place where they won't be able to hurt anyone ever again."

"You are safe now," Judith tells the boys.

"So are you," Hal says softly.

"Boys," the queen says, "We are delighted to have you home, and we owe you our lives."

"Tell ya what," LB says with his mouth full of tacos. "Another plate of these things and we'll call it even."

The trunks of fairy dust are lowered into the courtyard. Judith, Eldon and Elsie correct it's charge, turning it back to magical golden powder.

"Chloe, there you are. We are sorry about before," Elsie tells me with wide eyes. "Eldon had a moment."

"It's fine."

"Elsie," Judith calls sweetly. She and Eldon are standing over the fairy dust, about to cast a spell.

"Come see me after the party." Elsie tells me with urgency before she rushes to over them.

Glistening fairy dust sweeps through the courtyard magically changing the party scene into an elaborate gala with a long table piled with more delicious smelling food. The guys make a beeline for it. Peter follows them, hoping not to get caught with the king's treats.

Mrs. B cuts through the pack of people and stops in front of Jayce and I. "Jayson?" she cries.

"Mom!" he exclaims. She throws her arms around him. Jayce melts into her hug and the huge weight he had been forced to carry lifts off his shoulders. Mrs. B pulls me in and just holds us both lovingly.

Later at sunset, I sneak away to think and sit on the edge of the palace roof, watching the crowd. Some of the guys have eaten so much they are laying down, staring at the sky. Others are engaged in joyous conversation and laughter. Some of the wranglers have joined the band and Oldman Cooley is crooning a special song to Mrs. B.

My thoughts drown the sound to silence. I still have so many questions. I decide to focus on the positive facts.

The last prophecy turned out to be false for me. Or at least I changed my fate. I had played a part in the escape of the lost Shadow Boys, the demise of the wicked witch of the Heatherworld and the capture of her mercenary army – and in spite of what the ancient writings predicted, I survived.

I learned that I am not going insane, I am just coming into some intuition-type powers that I didn't know I had and I've done fairly well using them. I choose to forget about the whole controlling black magic by mere thought thing and the notion that my body encompasses equal positive and negative energies which cancel each other out and therefore I don't carry a charge.

No. More importantly, we have boys in our town... This is going to be interesting. Tash looks at me differently than he ever did before, and Jayce, well, Jayce is different. It is like he understood me before we'd even met—and he doesn't judge me. He accepts me just as I am, and even seems to like me that way. And kissing... kissing is very nice. I really want to do that again. My thoughts drift.

Out of the blue I hear, *"I am your mother."* A woman is standing in front of me, but I can't see her. There is a blur between us. Am I doing that? The haze surrounding me grows darker as the sound of thundering footsteps grows louder, echoing through the sky. It sounds like horse hooves pounding, POUNDING... I am whisked under the sound, into a pocket in time. Something touches my hand gently, like a whisper. I am in bright white light. All I can see is glistening shine. Then a figure moves in front of me.

"Chloe."

It is the Queen. She is smiling at me and holding my hands in hers.

"Mother?"

"I am so proud of you. I love you. I am so sorry for what you have had to endure."

I have so many questions, but I feel rushed, like something is wrong.

"You are my mother?"

"Yes, darling. But, it is still not safe, for either of us," she says worriedly, although with such love in her eyes. I haven't seen that before. It feels nice. She continues, *"You must not tell anyone who you are, and you must pretend you do not know me, for now. They are looking for me. Only a few loyal friends knew that your father and I had twins. They may have found your brother."*

"My brother? Peter is my brother. What do you mean found him...isn't he here?" I wondered outloud.

"I am not sure. That boy may be an ai synthetic. She tears up. *I feel a void in him. I am so worried."*

"Who is looking for you? Father?"

"Your father is, was, is no longer with us. Darling, he loved you very much. I know you must have so many questions. I wish we had more time. Your father was Lord Darkshadow. I am Queen of the Light. Our love was doomed from the start. Some beings do not want the lines blurred. You and your brother are a threat. We are looking for him now, but they do not know about you."

"Who are you afraid of?"

"Your uncle has always been jealous of your father's power. If he has Peter...She pauses, thinking. "Your uncle is a very bad influence." I feel her fading. *"Stay away from the elderfairies and anyone that can read you."*

She gazes at me sadly. *"We have been in here too long. I must go. Keep your mind clear, darling."*

I open my eyes, whispering "Keep my mind clear."

Tash is smiling at me. "That should be easy for you," he laughs. "You were squirming like a fish. I was going to wake you but you were funny."

"Great," I use as much grace as I can standing up. My legs are wobbly. Was that a dream or was it real? That is a lot to process. I am afraid to even think about it. It makes me sort of shudder.

Below me, in the courtyard, the Queen mingles with the townspeople. She glances up to see us on the roof, but with the same reaction one would make in looking a bird... normal. Like I don't matter to her. Maybe my dream was just a dream.

Peter is fake smiling at the gaggle of girls surrounding him as he tries futilely to lose them in the crowd. If he's a clone, it's a good one. He looks totally normal.

He flies up to the rooftop to take refuge among the boys scattered about, watching the horizon as they experience their first sunset.

"I never thought I'd see this day," Tash says softly.

The sky saturates with a palette of colors on fluffy clouds and streams of light.

"I did." LB says. "I didn't imagine it would be this pretty, though."

Tash sits on the ledge beside me. He is still wearing the shirt and dress pants, but is barefoot.

"I owe you an apology," he says sweetly. "It wasn't that I doubted you. I didn't want to lose you."

"You don't have to protect me anymore, you know."

"I don't know how to stop."

Jayce glances at us from the other edge of the roof.

"You like him." Tash says.

"I like all the guys, you too."

"You know what I mean."

"Why do I feel awkward talking to you about Jayce? Yeah. There is something special between us. But, it's not like you want me, right? You told me straight out, you are not my boyfriend."

I wait for him to respond. He is definitely holding back. The bond I feel with Tash is strong, and whenever he touches me or holds me, it warms my heart—but he put a wall between us a long time ago.

He gently strokes my hand then holds it. "That's not the way it can be with us."

I know he wants to kiss me. He draws closer, then glances at Jayce, kind of like he is giving him the okay.

Jayce doesn't waste a minute. He vanishes then, surprises us from behind reaching out his hand for me.

Tash looks down and Jayce sweeps me up in his arms.

A shooting star passes over us. It catches my attention when it slows above the palace, but when Jayce kisses me everything else fades away.

Moments later, in the northern tower of the Twisted Castle pale bejeweled hands pick up the pieces of the two broken wands and fuse them together as one. Then, with a flip of his cape, the blond man is gone.

FOLLOW
@debbiebishop

See more books and comic books
by Debbie Bishop at
www.debbiebishop.com

Made in the USA
Columbia, SC
22 November 2024

47320524R00143